DARK WATER

Laura McNeal

DARK WATER

Alfred A. Knopf
New York

THIS IS A BORZOI BOOK PUBLISHED BY ALFRED A. KNOPF

All rights reserved. Published in the United States by Alfred A. Knopf,
an imprint of Random House Children's Books, a division of Random House, Inc., New York.

Knopf, Borzoi Books, and the colophon are registered trademarks of Random House, Inc.

Visit us on the Web! www.randomhouse.com/teens

Educators and librarians, for a variety of teaching tools, visit us at
www.randomhouse.com/teachers

Library of Congress Cataloging-in-Publication Data
McNeal, Laura.
Dark water / Laura McNeal. — 1st ed.
p. cm.
Summary: Living in a cottage on her uncle's Southern California avocado ranch
since her parents' messy divorce, fifteen-year-old Pearl DeWitt meets and falls in love
with an illegal migrant worker, and is trapped with him when wildfires
approach his makeshift forest home.
ISBN 978-0-375-84973-2 (trade) — ISBN 978-0-375-94973-9 (lib. bdg.)
ISBN 978-0-375-89720-7 (e-book)
[1. Wildfires—Fiction. 2. Illegal aliens—Fiction. 3. Homeless persons—Fiction.
4. Divorce—Fiction. 5. Cousins—Fiction. 6. Family life—California—Fiction.
7. California—Fiction.] I. Title.
PZ7.M47879365Dar 2010
[Fic]—dc22
2009043249

The text of this book is set in 11.5-point Goudy.

Printed in the United States of America
September 2010
10 9 8 7 6 5 4 3 2 1
First Edition

For Tom

DARK WATER

One

You wouldn't have noticed me before the fire unless you saw that my eyes, like a pair of socks chosen in the dark, don't match. One is blue and the other's brown, a genetic trait called heterochromia that I share with white cats, Catahoula hog dogs, and water buffaloes. My uncle Hoyt used to tell me, when I was little, that it meant I could see fairies and peaceful ghosts.

Then I met Amiel, and for six months it seemed true what he whispered in his damaged voice: *Tú eres de dos mundos.*

He was wrong, of course. You can only belong to one world at a time.

Now that he's gone, I try to see things when I'm alone. I put one hand over my blue eye, and I look south. With my brown eye I can see all the way to Mexico. I fly over freeways and tile roofs and malls and swimming pools. I cross the Sierra de Juárez

Mountains and the Sea of Cortés to the place where Amiel was born, and I find the turquoise house with a red door. There are three chairs on the covered patio: one for him, one for me, and one for Uncle Hoyt. I tell myself the chairs are empty because we're not there yet. I watch for as long as I can and when my eye starts to water, I remove my hand.

Tomorrow, I'll look again.

Two

People move to Fallbrook, California, because it's sunny 340 days of the year. They move here to grow petunias and marigolds and palms and cycads and cactus and self-propagating succulents and blood oranges and Meyer lemons and sweet limes and, above all, avocados. They move here to grow them, I should say, or to pick them for other people.

The houses are far apart when you're out in the hills, where trees and petunias grow in straight lines for profit, but once you get close to town, the streets look like something drawn by a child with an Etch A Sketch. No overall plan, no sidewalks, just driveways going off in crazy lines that lead to other driveways, where signs point to other dead-end streets named in Spanish or English with no particular theme—*La Oreja Place* sticking out of *Rodeo Queen Drive* leading to

Tecolote Avenue, which if it were a sentence would read "the Ear on the Rodeo Queen of the Owl."

The ear and the queen and the owl are overrun with bougainvillea, ivy geraniums, tulip vines, and star jasmine, and that's what makes Fallbrook beautiful from a distance but tangled and confusing up close. It's a place where you can get lost no matter how long you've lived here, and there are only two roads out, something we didn't think much about before the fires began.

Three

I first saw Amiel de la Cruz Guerrero on the corner of one of those Etch A Sketch streets, where Alvarado meets Stage Coach. I was fifteen and he was seventeen, although he told employers he was twenty. I was in my sophomore year of high school and my mother was substitute-teaching because my father had left us, and as my mother was constantly saying over the phone when she thought I wasn't listening, *The wolf is at the door.*

Every weekday morning at seven-thirty we'd leave my uncle's avocado ranch, where we were living free of rent (but not shame) in the guesthouse. My mother would drink her coffee in the car while she drove, and I would eat dry Corn Pops from a Tupperware bowl. Traffic would bunch up as all the cars going to all the schools had to inch through the same four-way stop at Alvarado and Stage Coach, one corner of which was a day-labor gathering site, meaning Mexican and Guatemalan men would stand around on the empty lot hoping to get a day's work digging trenches, moving furniture, hauling firewood, or picking fruit. The men stared intensely into every car, hoping to win you over before you stopped. *Pick me,* their faces said. *The wolf is at the door.*

But on this morning, the men had their backs to the road. Our car rolled slowly to the stop sign, going even slower than usual because the drivers of the cars were staring, too.

When we got close enough, I could see a lanky guy in a flannel shirt and work pants doing some sort of act. Fallbrook calls itself the Avocado Capital of the World, so you don't live here without seeing guys pick avocados. Mostly it's done on high ladders, but there's also this funky tool like a lacrosse stick with a six-foot handle. You stick the pole way up in the tree, hook the avocado, yank, then lower the pole so you can drop the fruit into a huge canvas bag you're wearing slung over one shoulder and across your chest. That's what Amiel was doing that morning, only without the pole, the sack, the tree, or the avocado.

"What in the world?" my mom asked.

"He's picking imaginary fruit," I said.

She snuck a look. "That's the oddest thing I've ever seen."

"Can we hire him?"

She snorted. It was our turn to dart through the intersection just as Amiel de la Cruz Guerrero touched his imaginary avocado-picking pole to a live electrical wire and received an imaginary jolt, which made all the day-labor guys laugh.

Four

The next day, he was juggling three actual, not mimed, soda bottles. "Look, Mom," I said, so she peered over for a second.

"I hope he doesn't litter," she said.

"That sounded kind of racist."

"There's no trash can on this corner, if you haven't noticed. And the neighbors will make a stink if junk starts piling up."

The day after that, Amiel was standing on his head. While I watched, the guy next to him gave his feet a shove and he tipped over. "I guess the other guys think he's showing off too much," I said.

My mother sighed. "It could be he's in the wrong field for his talents."

On Friday, the boy just stood there, hands in his pockets like the rest of the men. He didn't even look into our car like the others did. "Why do they come here?" I asked my mom.

"I don't know why they pick this corner," she said.

"I mean cross the border."

"To work."

"But they clearly don't have work."

"The hope of work," she said.

That's when I thought of Hoyt. My uncle Hoyt grew so many avocados that he had to employ people year-round to fertilize, water, pick, prune, and patrol fences to keep thieves from stealing bins of fruit worth thousands of dollars, a crime called—I'm not kidding—"Grand Theft Avocado." All of his employees were Mexican. I asked him about it once, why every farmworker you ever saw in Fallbrook was Hispanic.

"I don't know who picks corn in Iowa or lingonberries in Sweden," Hoyt said, "but white teenage boys don't pick avocados in California. Neither do grown white men. Not enough money in it for them. Or status."

I didn't ask if his guys were legal, because I knew generally who was and who wasn't. The legal ones had drivers' licenses. They could go home to Mexico on planes and come back on planes. The illegal ones worked seven days a week for years at a stretch, saved their money, then went home for about eight months to be with their families. Every time they went home, they had to borrow money to pay coyotes who smuggled them back in.

"Do you think they're happy, the workers?" I asked. You could ask Hoyt questions like that and he wouldn't get defensive.

"I'll tell you a story," Hoyt said. "You know Esteban, right?

His kids and wife are here because he has papers. He brought them legally about ten years ago. That was when I was building Robby's tree house." My cousin Robby. "I took Esteban's kids up into the tree house because I thought they'd like to play in it. And you know what his youngest kid said? He looked around with this really serious face and asked, 'Who's going to live here?'"

Robby's tree house was pretty nice, with cedar shingles on the outside and two framed windows and a peaked roof, but there was no electricity or plumbing or even a door, and it was about eight feet square.

"That's because," Hoyt went on, "in the village where they were born, plenty of people lived in places worse than that tree house. I'll tell you what, Pearl. I'm going to take you and Robby with me to Esteban's village in Mexico next time I go. I want you to see why he left."

On Friday after school, I decided to ask Hoyt if he ever hired guys from the street corner. I found him standing in his driveway, shaking his head in frustration while Esteban talked in Spanish on a cell phone. Esteban kept saying the same phrases over and over again, and I didn't know what they meant, but I could tell he was calming somebody down.

"What's the matter?" I asked Hoyt when Esteban had gone away.

"They've deported one of my guys."

"How did they get him?"

It was a mystery to me how the border patrol made decisions. There were lots of day-labor pickup points like the corner where I'd seen Amiel, and those places didn't change much, so you'd think agents would know right where to go.

"He was at the grocery store," Hoyt said.

"Does that happen a lot?"

"It didn't used to," Hoyt said.

"What will happen now?"

"We'll get the money together to help him cross again, which means about four thousand dollars, or he'll give up and go home."

"So . . . ," I said, stalling until I could think of the right words. "Do you need any help in the meantime?"

"Why? Can you prune avocados?"

"Well, maybe, but I was thinking of someone you could hire."

"Who?"

I didn't know Amiel's name yet, and I fumbled for a way to make a juggling mime sound employable. "This guy I saw at the corner of Stage Coach. You know, where they gather when they want work."

Hoyt looked amused. "What, is he handsome?"

"No. I mean, that's not why." I told Hoyt about the mime routine and the headstand. "He just seemed unusual is all. And I feel sorry for those guys. They have it the worst, don't they?"

"They're probably bad workers or they drink too much. If they were good workers," Hoyt said, "their friends and relatives would recommend them and they'd have jobs."

"What if you don't have any friends or relatives here?"

"They all do, Pearl."

"But how? Somebody has to be first, right?"

Hoyt just looked at me. "Technically, yeah. But everyone I hire is recommended by a cousin, a brother, an uncle, or a friend. It works better that way."

It reminded me of the riddles my dad used to ask me at dinner:

What can you catch but not throw?

A cold.

What goes around the world but stays in the corner?

A stamp.

If nobody knows you, how do you ever get a job?

To this I had no answer.

Five

Sometimes on Saturdays, if Hoyt had errands to run in town, he'd talk Robby and me into going with him in exchange for a donut, and that's what he did the next morning.

It was late spring, meaning April, and the look of everything just about made you happy even if your father was a louse. The wild grass that had sprouted after the winter rains (my favorite two months of the whole year) had not yet turned to evil poky foxtails that drill into your socks and shoelaces. Most of the hills were a heartbreaking velvety green, and the others, where fruit trees had been stumped and painted white, looked like brown quilts knotted with white yarn.

I would have gone with Hoyt even if no donuts were involved. I loved riding in his truck because it was an old Ford with bench seats. It smelled like dirt, coffee, grease, and the scratchy wool Indian blanket that covered the front seat.

Robby and I called it the Ford Packrat because the foot wells were filled with irrigation tubing, receipts dating to 1985, hamburger wrappers, and rusty iron tools. We had plans to market something called the Ford Packrat XC80 if Robby pursued his planned career in industrial design.

My cousin Robby no longer speaks to me and is living in Cambridge, Massachusetts, starting his second year at MIT.

On the day in question, though, that beautiful, green-grass day, I sat in the middle and angled my knees toward Robby. Robby at sixteen was tall and ethereal-looking, like his mother, my aunt Agnès, pronounced *Aun-yez*, not the American way. She was born and raised in France, a point of superiority to her way of thinking that made it hard for all of us, except Robby and Hoyt, to do anything but tolerate her. Robby played the clarinet and scored outrageously high on college tests and ran track and collected these cute but obscure figurines no one in America had ever heard of, which depicted the comic-book adventures of a bald-headed kid named Tintin and his white terrier, Snowy. I scored pretty high in English because, thanks to my mom, I read all the time, but Robby was the acknowledged genius in our family.

First we drove to Miller Pipe and hung around while my uncle picked out whatever pipe fittings he needed for the grove, and then we rode in all that sunshine to the Donut Palace, a tiny store lacquered in yellow Formica that was owned and ferociously sanitized by a Taiwanese family. I always got a chocolate-glazed, Robby always got a jelly-filled, and Uncle Hoyt always got a sugar twist. Hoyt could take or leave the sugar twist, to be honest, but he hated to go anywhere by himself.

I was still nibbling on my chocolate-glazed when we rolled up to the four-way stop at Alvarado and Stage Coach, and Amiel was in his usual spot, juggling nothing and looking depressed. "That's him!" I told my uncle. "The mime I told you about!"

"Keep driving," Robby said with his usual semi-irritating authority. "We should close the borders to all mimes. And clowns. And folk dancers."

Amiel, so graceful and brown and lean, was wearing a loose T-shirt and jeans, so he didn't exactly have that I'm-a-mime look about him. To my surprise, Hoyt slowly swung the Packrat onto the dirt. Five men swarmed the truck right away, clapping their chests, gripping the doors, and shouting in English and Spanish until you hated yourself. They called Hoyt "Señor" and "Mister."

"*Uno momentito,*" Hoyt said to the workers, his stock phrase, and I looked kind of desperately at Amiel, hoping he'd somehow impress my uncle.

"That one," I said.

Amiel saw me, so he pointed to himself with an extra-long, extra-expressive finger. He raised one eyebrow. He looked in an exaggerated way behind him.

"Oh my God," Robby said. "If he gets into a box, I'm going to shoot myself."

The mime walked slowly toward the pickup, which was angled so that he was approaching Robby's side. Hoyt patted Robby's knee and said, "Roll down your window, Rob."

14

It was that kind of truck, where you had to roll, so Robby did, but very slowly. "This is not worth a donut," he muttered.

"You know how to use a chain saw?" my uncle called out Robby's window at Amiel.

All the other men were still holding Hoyt's door like they were in deep water and we were a boat. "¡Sí! Chain saw!" they said, but Hoyt was still looking out Robby's window at the boy who was now six inches from me.

He was slender to the point of bony, with a smooth, narrow, mournful face. His eyes were a lighter shade of brown than his skin, like gold sand in a river bottom, and his nose might have seemed large if his eyes hadn't been so arresting. In contrast to his straightness and tautness, his hair seemed uncontrollably curly.

Amiel held one hand in the shape of a C, a gesture I later learned was his gesture for "sí." He strapped an imaginary pair of goggles over his creek-glitter eyes. He pulled on an imaginary cord and started up an imaginary chain saw. He shuddered and appeared unable to control the weight of it, then nodded to himself and smiled at us before starting to cut through an invisible tree limb. He stopped the chain saw and picked up the imaginary log and presented it to us.

Uncle Hoyt laughed. Robby groaned. The other men, the ones at Hoyt's window, made disgusted noises and looked angry enough that I knew things would be worse for Amiel if Hoyt just drove away.

But he didn't. "What the hell. Hop in!" Hoyt said, then he nodded at the oldest man hanging around his door handle, a guy who couldn't have been more than four and a half feet tall under his black cowboy hat, and said, "You too, señor." I felt extremely happy and was full of affection for my uncle. I just knew he wouldn't be sorry.

The very small old man and Amiel climbed into the narrow backseat.

"What's your name?" Hoyt asked.

The tiny vaquero said he was called Gallo, and Amiel handed us a not entirely clean business card that said AMIEL DE LA CRUZ GUERRERO. HARD WORKER.

"Are you deaf?" Hoyt asked him, returning the card to Amiel.

Amiel shook his head and pointed to his throat.

"Well, *mucho gusto!*" Hoyt said, another of his stock Spanish phrases, and Robby looked like he was figuring out how fast he would have to roll if he jumped out of a truck going thirty miles per hour.

"Where are you from?" Hoyt practically shouted in Spanish to the old vaquero in the back. The truck was loud with the windows down, sunshine and wind whipping us all, the motor roaring. But it wasn't just that. Uncle Hoyt, like just about everyone else, spoke louder in a foreign language, and I think he still thought Amiel was deaf. Bougainvillea flew by.

"Acapulco," the old man said beautifully, like it was the name of a love song.

"This is my son, Roberto," my uncle announced real slow and loud, and Robby shrank into the door. "I'm Hoyt, okay?"

he went on. Then he added, "This pretty señorita here is my niece, Pearl!"

"You daughter?" the old one asked in English.

"*Sobrina*," Hoyt said.

"*Sí*," the vaquero said. "*Sí. Sobrina.*"

By this time we were crossing the freeway to Rainbow, population 2,026, elevation 1,043. Rainbow had its own elementary school, café, gas station, and fruit stand but was otherwise just a strung-out collection of ranches, packinghouses, nurseries, and farms. Huge boulders were clumped in all the hills like brown sugar that's gone hard on you, and lilacs and oak trees grew crooked and wild in their shade.

Six months from this day, a fire would leap from east to west, from Rainbow to Fallbrook. Eight lanes is a lot of concrete for a fire to cross, and I would have told you there was no way it could ever happen. In spring, everything is so conk-you-in-the-head pretty. Painted lady butterflies kept fluttering past the windshield, the air smelled like orange blossoms, and Amiel was in the backseat. I understood exactly why people wrote musicals.

We turned and headed toward the gate that Uncle Hoyt welded in adult education classes before Robby or I was born.

"Here we are," he said, steering us under the sign that said LEMON DROP RANCH in loopy iron letters. When I was little, he would always sing, *Where troubles melt like lemon drops, away above the chimney tops, that's where you'll find me.*

In Rainbow, see.

We drove under the arch, gravel popping under the tires of Hoyt's truck as I moved into the future, where I would be Perla and Amiel would sign my name by opening the oyster shell of his two hands and extracting a small invisible pearl, his long expressive fingers turning into a nest and then a bird, undulating so that you forgot his hand was a hand at all.

Six

My mother and I lived uneasily that year in my uncle's guest-house, the oldest structure in Rainbow. The cottage was the original homestead of a pioneer named Lavar Mulveen, who came to Rainbow in the thirties to raise olives but ended up planting alligator pears, an early, fanciful name for avocados. I hated Lavar's rusty bathtub and dysfunctional toilet, but I liked how the porch was a big extra room, which my mom and I had fitted out with an old wicker sofa and a lamp and even a needlepoint rug that Robby and I bought at a garage sale for three dollars. Everything that reminded us of my dad we pitched: his sports memorabilia (not true that you can get a fortune for old baseball cards), his record albums, his ultra-lux leather sofa, his ultra-lux glass-and-steel office furniture, the model train layout his dad built and which was like a tiny green kingdom in our garage when I was little, complete with creeks and forests and bridges and houses and barns. We smashed it to pieces, my mother and I. I was King Kong and she was Godzilla. In case that seems slightly hysterical, I'll tell you how he left.

It was a Friday in January, and on this particular Friday we were expecting my father to fly home from Phoenix, where he was turning apartments into condos, something you can't do in a farm town like Fallbrook. He'd be gone for about a month at a time, and for those weeks it was like my mom and I were roommates. We never made our beds and we didn't keep to any kind of a schedule and we watched girl movies after I finished my homework, and then my dad flew in and we cleaned everything up and my mom cooked fancy food and it was like they were dating each other in the type of movie we liked best.

At least, I thought that's the kind of movie it was until I came home from Greenie's on January 12. I'd made my bed in the morning, and the night before I'd helped clean the bathrooms and iron napkins and pick popcorn bits out of the lux leather sofa. I knew my mother was making lobster Newburg and bananas Foster. I knew she'd bought a new dress at Talbots because I helped pick it out.

I came into the house, the one on Macadamia Drive with a stained glass window of a hummingbird by the front door, and I saw that my mom had left pots and pans and food all over the kitchen. "Mom?" I said.

She was sitting extra still on the couch, like taxidermy. It's hard to describe her because a parent is so close it's like trying to see the glasses you have on. But she was a spunky, forty-five-year-old version of the woman in the wedding picture. She still had long blond hair and blue eyes that matched and tanned freckly skin and the sort of cheerleader nose I didn't inherit. She wasn't as thin as she used to be or as my father seemed to want, but she still looked nice in the linen dresses and blousy shirts she liked to wear. What was odd, at this moment, was that she was not even looking at anything. Normally, if my mother was sitting, she was reading a ten-thousand-page biography of Thomas Hardy or folding laundry. Not staring at the empty fireplace.

"What's wrong?" I asked.

No sign that she'd even heard me.

"Did you make gooseberry pie again?" I asked, going for humor. My mother is an impulsive overdoer who gets her feelings hurt a lot. When I was in second grade, she made me a Pilgrim's dress for Thanksgiving complete with white cap, and then I had to wear it to school. When I was in third grade, instead of buying cupcakes at the grocery store like everyone else, she made petit fours decorated with pink French buttercream frosting—not pink because she squeezed a little bottle of red dye but because she boiled beets in water and made her own natural dye, which naturally none of the eight-year-olds appreciated. And once, she read a short story by Chekhov about this Russian guy named Ivan Ivanovitch who'd wanted all his life to eat his own gooseberries, so he bought a farm and planted the berry bushes and tended them like they were his little babies for what seemed like a century, but once he finally, finally tasted the gooseberries, they were sour—nothing could live up to his dream of the fruit. That's the story. It's all pointing to this moment when the fruit falls short of the *memory* of fruit. But my mom bought some canned gooseberries, the only kind you can get in California, and she made a gooseberry pie. (Gooseberries, if you don't know, look like grapes, but they're horrible.) I wouldn't eat the pie, and neither would my father. It was a big letdown for her, even though I pointed out that this was the most Chekhovian result possible.

My mother sat dangerously still on the couch in her Talbots dress and her high-heeled shoes and didn't answer me.

"I thought Dad was going to be here," I said.

No movement from the couch.

"Was there a plane wreck?"

She shook her head.

"Are you sitting like that because Dad was killed?" I asked. I couldn't imagine anything worse than that.

She shook her head.

"Is someone else dead or hurt?"

More head shaking.

There's this finger game my mom made up when I was little, a variation on "Here is the church, here is the steeple" or "Where is Thumbkin?" My mom figured out that when I wouldn't talk to her, I would talk to "Mrs. Nelson," which was just her thumb popped up between her curved fingers. Mrs. Nelson the Living Thumb sat there like a grandma tucked into her covers and talked me through things like the extraction of a rod from my wrist and third-grade recorder concerts and throwing up on the bus during a field trip to Birch Aquarium.

Feeling pretty stupid, but also certain that something had set the world on a diagonal so steep everything in it was about to go sliding and crashing to pieces, I let my thumbnail poke up through my fist and I set the fist on her knee.

I wiggled my thumbnail like it was a friendly earthworm.

My mother looked at the thumb and said, in a very slow and controlled voice, as if she were issuing instructions for bomb-defusing, "Your dad was here. He said he doesn't love me anymore. He hasn't loved me for ten years. He's going to live in Phoenix now."

I pulled my thumb back out because I was so shocked, and Mrs. Nelson disappeared for good. I think I couldn't stand for Mrs. Nelson to know what had happened to us.

For reasons I can't explain to you because at the time it just seemed like our fate, my father didn't have to keep paying the mortgage on our four-bedroom, three-and-a-half-bath Spanish ranch. We were what my mother called "upside down" on the house, which means you owe the bank more than it's worth. That was because my father had refinanced the house to get the money for the project in Phoenix that was now, somehow, only in his name. So we sold things. We sold the $2,500 living room set my dad had picked out a few years earlier. We sold the extra freezer, the sofa bed, and the extra television. In each case, we were upside down. Little by little we gave away or sold or threw out everything, and I imagined it all falling through the air as our house turned upside down. In time all we had were old quilts, my grandmother's Singer sewing machine, one-tenth of my mom's and my books (because there were way too many of them to keep in Lavar's house), and four boxes of Christmas ornaments. One night when I went to the movies with Robby (I remember what we saw—the Clause movie where Santa has to find a wife), my mother got drunk, which she never, never did normally, and smashed all the smashable Christmas ornaments with a croquet mallet. Then she burned her wedding pictures in the Weber grill.

A realtor who used to work with my dad sold the house, which I liked to picture with the pointed part of the roof as a balancing point and the door up high, so that nobody could get in. We didn't get any money afterward.

Seven

Which is why Robby and I were sitting in Lavar's decrepit cottage on Amiel's first day of work. I put some tuna on the counter, opened it, and stared out the window. I carried around for the first time that day the sensation of Amiel being nearby, like he had one of those laser pointers aimed at me and the red dot of light moved wherever I moved. All I could see through the window, though, were avocado trunks and a couple of crows.

"Want some *le* crackers?" I asked.

Robby was sniffing the tuna like it had gone bad. He doesn't look like my blood relative at all, which I guess is normal for cousins. He has his mother's coloring, which is whitish, and black hair and gray eyes. His lips are just ridiculously pretty—kind of salmon and curvy the way a woman's might be, but he's got a square jaw, blocky hands, and buff shoulders, so he doesn't look like a wuss who collects Tintin figures.

"I just made it *le* yesterday," I said. It was a thing we started doing back when our mothers got this idea that Robby and I should speak to each other *exclusively* in French, rendering me totally fluent and chic by, like, second grade and keeping Robby from the dreadful fate of growing up American. Robby was much better at Franglish than I was and could generally do more than *"le"* the heck out of things, but he wasn't in the mood.

"What's that terrible smell?" Robby said. He was looking through his glasses in a moderately disgusted way at my mother's silkworms. My mom's best friend, Louise Bart, gave my mom the worms because she noticed, while visiting us in our new old cottage, that my uncle had a pair of mulberry trees. A normal friend might have found this a great opportunity to make mulberry cobbler (which tastes like blackberry cobbler), but this friend, like my mother, is fatally interesting, so she said, "You could raise silkworms here!"

"We could?" I asked. "Why?"

"Because you have a constant source of food for them," she said. "Full-grown mulberry trees."

I meant "why would we *want* to," but my mother didn't need to ask. She'd gone with Louise to workshops on raising your own cotton, she'd learned to use a spindle one year, and she saw herself, I think, raising silkworms, processing the silk, and weaving it into priceless cloth that she could sell when the wolf came to the door.

Robby looked dubiously at the smooth white caterpillars crawling on the mattress of mulberry leaves my mother and I fetched for them three times a day. They munched big lacy holes until their pulsing bodies were strewn with green crumbs, then waited to be covered again, like children who have kicked off their blankets.

"Aren't you worried they'll crawl into your Caesar salad?" he asked.

"No," I said, "they've been bred not to wander," which is what my mother told me.

"You'd think they might try that with people," he said more bitterly than I would have thought normal. He stared at them a little longer. "They smell kind of funky."

"Don't we all," I said. I was pretty sure the house smelled funky all by itself, before we even moved in. "But they're interesting, don't you think?" I asked. Now that the caterpillars had molted into newer, larger skins five times, they were as big as my index finger and snowy white. A black line that looked like an artery pulsed just below the skin along their backs like the soft spot of a newborn baby's head. "Do you hear that?" I asked.

Robby slumped without interest on the sofa back. "What?"

"Can't you hear it?" It was a crackly-tap-tappy sound. I'd once thought it was the sound of twenty-five mouths chomping mulberry leaves, but it turned out to be all their little caterpillar feet grasping and ungrasping the leaves as they moved.

"Snap, crackledy, pop," Robby said finally. "That is kind of creepily interesting. I recommend checking your cereal bowl before you eat in the morning."

I was disappointed that he didn't appreciate the caterpillars, but I couldn't really blame him. Not everyone likes a tray of devouring insects in the living room.

"I think I'll go eat something at home," Robby said.

"Well, why don't you," I said. "You big snob."

"Stop calling me that." But he didn't leave. He just stretched full length on the sofa, which wasn't easy because of the various pillows and magazines and remote controls that had been strewn all over it, and he put his arm across his forehead in this way that at first looked stupidly theatrical. But then he said in this seriously miserable voice, *"Cherchez la femme."*

"Cherchez la what?"

"It's just this French saying. If a guy's behaving weirdly, look for the woman." His face was whiter than usual, and sadder.

"Are you hiding a *le* woman somewhere?"

"No," he said. "It's my *le* dad. He has a *le femme.*"

It was a joking way to put it, but the air in the room had changed. It was all prickly and electrified now, like a wire. I didn't pick up the tuna or finish opening the box of crackers.

"How do you know?"

"Because I *caught* him," Robby said.

Eight

He said it happened two weeks ago when his mother was on her way to Paris and his dad was supposedly gunning his motorbike on trails. Robby wasn't supposed to be home, either, because the Redlands Symphony orchestra was performing in the auditorium at the high school, and Robby, as a band member, was an usher who was going to audition afterward for a spot at the music camp the conductor was involved with somehow. Except that Robby got all the way to the high school, which is a twenty-minute drive from the ranch, and discovered he forgot the reeds for his clarinet. The band teacher is this cranky bearded man named Mr. Van der Does who is always telling Robby that what stands between Robby and success is a lack of commitment, because Mr. Van der Does, like my father, believes that disorganization is a sign that you don't really care.

So Robby drove back to the ranch, trying to hurry so that at least he could hear the second half of the concert and do his audition, and he left the Ford Packrat parked on the dirt road that led from the house to the grove because he thought that'd be quicker. When he ran up the hill to the house, he noticed a strange car, but he didn't give it a lot of thought—there was no extra parking for the guesthouse, so if somebody came to visit me or my mom, they parked in Robby's driveway. So Robby opened the front door and went up the stairs to his room for the reeds, and then he looked in the mirror and saw that he'd sweated completely through his only white shirt. His room was next to his father and mother's bedroom, and he decided to borrow one of his dad's shirts, but the bedroom door was shut.

"It's never shut during the day," Robby said. "They don't ever close it except at night when they go to bed."

It struck him as odd, so Robby stood there for a second. He knocked. He heard noises—not voices, but shifting noises. His dad opened the door just a crack and came out, closing the door behind him. "Hey, what's up?" he asked.

"I forgot my reeds," Robby said. "I thought you went out on a ride."

"I got a flat tire," his father said.

"Can I borrow a white shirt? I got this one all sweaty, and I'm really late."

Robby waited for Hoyt to open the bedroom door and walk into the room with Robby, get the shirt out of the closet, and hand it to him. But his father didn't open the door. He stood in front of it like a bad actor in a high school play. "Sure," Hoyt said. But he still didn't open the door.

"I'm really late," Robby repeated.

"I think my dress shirts are downstairs," Hoyt said. "In the laundry room."

Robby turned and went downstairs, and his dad followed him, but there weren't any shirts. "I thought your mother said she was going to iron them," his dad said.

"Never mind," Robby said. He walked out the front door, and he saw the strange car again. It was just an anonymous silver-green-gray Toyota, but he noticed the name—Avalon—because of our mock global launches of new cars: the Ford Estrogen, the Dodge Hootenany, the Honda Dust Bunny.

"Whose car is that, anyway?" Robby asked his dad. Hanging from the mirror was a red and white graduation tassel. Fallbrook High colors.

"I don't know," Hoyt said. "Maybe somebody visiting Pearl or Sharon."

Some people can lie, and some people can't. My father was a world-class liar, for instance. We never suspected a thing until the day of the Talbots dress. For some reason, though, Robby felt the off-ness of the conversation and looked hard into the Avalon as he walked past. He saw that the number on the tassel meant she'd graduated two years ago. He saw a sticker on the windshield that permitted the driver to park at Cal State San Marcos. He saw a tennis racket in the backseat. He said, "See ya," and ran down to the truck with the box of reeds in his hand.

"I decided I would just pretend to leave," he told me. "I would sneak back to the house and hide in the xylosma hedge and watch who got into that car. That's when I called you, remember?" he asked.

I broke a cracker in half and shook my head. I walked over to the desk calendar where my mother used to write down what days my father would be home and when my after-school art classes were and where she now wrote down appointments with the attorney, the forensic accountant, and the court-mandated psychiatrist. Sunday, April 15, was blank.

"You were at Major Market," Robby said. "You said your mother was asking Alfredo whether it was true that grocery stores throw away perfectly good produce."

Alfredo was the produce manager and he'd been sprucing those vegetable displays my whole life. "That's right," I said. I remembered standing far away from my mother behind the floral department, inhaling the scent of crushed carnations and wondering if my mother was going to start scavenging for food in Dumpsters.

"You were in a big hurry to get off the phone," Robby added. "So I did it."

"Did what?"

"Parked the truck and walked back to the house."

Robby was sitting up by this time and looking like the Greek god of unhappiness. He picked up one of my mother's wooden spindles and played with the fluffy bit of roving she was trying to turn into yarn.

"So you hid in the bushes?" I asked.

"Yeah. I sat in the hedge. For a while, it was like a desert island except the water pump was cycling on and off. Then I heard the front door and some high-heeled shoes."

"What did she look like?" I asked.

Pretty much anyone who's ever seen my aunt Agnès has remarked on her looks. The pink lips that Robby has are a direct gift from her, plus she has a stunning figure and sophisticated clothes of a kind you'd never buy around here and skin kept young by I don't know what kind of Parisian secret creams. What kind of man needs more than that?

Robby said he was too far away to see much, so he didn't know except that she seemed really young. "They kissed, which made me want to upchuck, and then she drove her Toyota Succubus away."

"It was a bus? I thought you said it was an Avalon."

Robby looked annoyed.

"Oh," I said. "I get it," though I didn't. I thought he'd made it up. Eventually, I came across the word in lit class and learned it's a medieval she-demon who seduces you when you sleep. "So you've got no idea who it was?"

"No, none, could hardly see her, like I said."

"Are you going to tell your mom?"

Robby shrugged. "It's hard to picture myself doing that. Would you be the one to *do* that to her?"

I'd never thought of myself as having the power to *do* anything to Agnès. "Are you going to ask your dad about it?"

Robby looked glumly at the spindle in his hand, the frayed bit of fluff. "I thought about it. I considered just bursting out of

the bushes like a policeman or something. '*Nobody move!
Hands in the air!*' "

"What *did* you do?" I was too hungry not to eat some tuna.
I scooped up the lukewarm stuff on a cracker and tried to chew
quietly. I can eat when I'm upset is the problem.

"Sat in the bushes awhile longer, then walked to the
truck."

"Did you miss the audition?"

"Yeah."

I didn't say anything. I knew he'd really, really wanted to
go to that camp. And Mr. Van der Does has a seriously long
memory. If you're two minutes late for a madrigal practice, you
can kiss your solos goodbye. But after my father left us, after we
found the receipts, after the forensic accountant did the math,
after eleven (repeat *eleven*) of my mother's friends said, "Is he
gay?" it was hard to care about madrigal solos. Sometimes it
was like my blood had turned to sand.

"Where'd you go?" I asked.

"You mean when I drove around?"

"Yeah." I thought he'd say the river. We started going there
when he first got his license, and it was what I was looking forward to when I turned sixteen, just driving over to the Santa
Margarita and hiking to the place where the river fans out
green and wide. I liked to walk down into the reeds and sit
with my bare feet in the cool shallow streams and watch the
tadpoles scoot around. I could spend a whole hour on the table
rock that splits the current in a wide bend of the river, crouching there like a bird and just listening to the water gurgle and

staring at the clear brown rocks all speckled and shiny under the surface. Spring was the best time because the willow fluff catches on the wind and snows itself through the air.

"I spoke to . . . this ostrich," Robby said, kind of sheepishly. He startled me out of my river thoughts. "Metaphorically?"

"I didn't mean it metaphorically."

"So you *literally* spoke to the ostrich?" We're both scornful of people who say they *literally* freaked out or they *literally* jumped out of their skins. I offered Robby a cracker lightly spread with tuna, but he shook his head, so I ate it. Robby touched his blocky fingertips together in this way he has. It's like one hand is a mirror image of the other hand: *tap, tap, tap.* All five fingers checking to see if the other five fingers still match.

"In that big pasture to the south of us," he said. "You know, the one you can see from the freeway?"

"Where the cows are sometimes?" It was a place I liked staring at from the car, actually, because it didn't have any houses on it or even a golf course, so it was soothingly au naturel.

"Yeah. There's this honest-to-God ostrich living there, too," he said.

"A talking ostrich?"

Robby lay back down on the sofa and closed his eyes. The silkworms sounded like Pop Rocks in an open mouth. "No. Not a *le* talking ostrich." He sounded deeply annoyed.

"No offense," I said. "*Pardonnez le moi.*" I ate another cracker and wished for coffee.

Robby started up again. "I was just driving along that frontage road, you know, planning how far I could go on a tank of gas and thinking I could hang out in Tijuana for a while, maybe busk my way down to Ecuador, and then I looked over and I thought, *No way. It can't be.* I pulled over and there's this ostrich. Right there by the fence. Staring at me with its big freaky eyes."

I wondered whether you could even busk yourself to the next town with classical clarinet, but I decided he was too touchy to be teased about that. "So what did you, um, say to it?"

"Nothing," Robby said. "Nightclub patter. *What's a girl like you doing in a place like this?*"

I hoped nightclub patter wasn't going to be part of his busking routine. "It was a girl?"

"No idea."

I started to make coffee. My mother says I'm going to stunt my growth and I say, *Good.* It keeps that feeling at bay, sometimes, the sand piling up in my veins. "Then what?"

"I guess I startled it. The *le* bird ran away."

"Maybe you could tame it. I think people used to ride ostriches, didn't they? In Africa or somewhere. Or maybe that was the Robinson Crusoe movie."

"I'm going to *le* fall asleep now," Robby said.

"You don't want any coffee?"

"Staying awake is the last thing I want," Robby said. "The very last thing."

So I unfolded a quilt and laid it over him and he didn't say a word, just turned his head deeper into the pillow like a little boy. I knew that feeling when you can't move your mouth anymore or your eyes. I poured coffee into a mug, added too much cream and too much sugar, and then poured another one and fixed it the same way. I knew who I was looking for and who I definitely didn't want to see. If I ran into my uncle, I knew he would look different to me now, as my dad did, and I hated, hated, *hated* that feeling. I supposed that was why Robby told me about it. You want someone else to share your bitterness at learning this person you've idolized your whole life is a big fat fabricator. Now I wanted to be with someone I couldn't even talk to, someone who didn't know anything about me or my family of unreliable men.

It was either the ostrich or Amiel, so I took one coffee in each hand.

Nine

The avocado grove looks nothing like it did that day. Nine hundred of Hoyt's trees burned in the Agua Prieta fire. Lavar Mulveen's white-shingled house, the needlepoint rug, the sofa, the three pictures I had saved of my father and me, the dish shaped like a heart that I made for him in sixth grade, the silverware, and every book we owned. Robby's Tintin figures. My mother's lock of her grandmother's hair. All burned. The wrought-iron fence melted, then hardened into a roller-coaster rail, and the prickly pear cactus that grew along the ridge liquefied and sank into ghastly skin-colored piles. But the avocado trees didn't completely die. The workers stumped every single one and painted them white. They replaced the sprinkler pipes that shriveled up like dead snakes, and they stacked the charred logs in neat pyramids beside the white, still-living trunks.

But on that April day the trees outside the guesthouse spread their green fluttering limbs high above my head. The leaves underfoot were copper-colored and the light was amber where the canopy broke apart and made an aperture for the sun. It wasn't too difficult to find Amiel, but it was hard to approach him. First of all, he was still working with Gallo, whom I totally forgot, and I hadn't brought three coffees. They turned at the sound of my feet crushing many layers of dried leaves. I held up both cups, and they nodded. They looked so hot and sweaty that I wondered why on earth I hadn't brought water, but if they wondered the same thing, they didn't say so. They leaned back on two different tree trunks and sipped. They didn't look at me or at each other. I could tell they were waiting for me to go away, which was normal. Why would I stay?

"Hot," I said in Spanish.

They nodded and Gallo said, "*Sí, caliente,*" though he might have thought I meant the coffee. I wished I knew the words for *How long have you been here?* or *What's wrong with your throat?*

I realized the obvious, finally: getting to know a mute person was going to be tricky. I forgot about my heterochromia, too. I forget about it more than you might think because it's not a limp or a missing finger or a port-wine stain on my arm. I can't *see* the eyes myself. I remembered my freakishness a half second after I realized that Amiel was looking into my eyes with searing interest.

"*¿De dónde eres?*" I managed to say.

"Acapulco," Gallo said, which of course he'd already said that morning.

Amiel pointed to his own matching eyes and then, gently, at mine.

Gallo nodded and studied me intently, as if making a medical diagnosis. He spoke to Amiel in Spanish, and I'd love to say that I translated every word in my head, but I just nodded pseudo-wisely until finally I gave up. "*¿Cómo?*" I said, which is Spanish for "Huh?"

Gallo pointed to my eyes again and then at the sun, or maybe the treetops. I understood the word for "cat" and the word for "worlds." I was like a cat of the world? I belonged in cat world? Amiel was looking at me with the kind of interest that made my mouth dry up. I was Braille and his eyes were fingers.

I guess there's not an easy way to mime "You are of two worlds," which is what Gallo said after he compared me to a cat. In the beginning, what I would do is memorize the sound of a Spanish phrase, and then I'd get someone at school to translate. Later, I learned words and grammar.

Amiel studied me for a second, and then he finished his coffee. He didn't say anything to me that day. It was a while after that, at the river, when Amiel said it over and over again to me slowly, in his damaged voice that is like a whisper: *Tú eres de dos mundos, tú eres de dos mundos, tú eres de dos mundos.*

Ten

I woke up at 1:15 a.m. to see my mother watching the silk-worms. I slept in the living room on a foldout couch, and she used the single bedroom that I guess was old Lavar's. Usually if I woke up in the middle of the night, she was in her bed with the light on, reading nonfiction paperbacks about women who start their lives over in canny new business ventures instead of the novels she used to like. But that night she was sitting on a kitchen chair by the tray of worms, wearing the peach chenille robe my father and I gave her on Mother's Day so many years ago that the sleeve is ripped at the armhole and the cuffs are dingy.

She looked over her cup of hot Postum at me. Postum is what the label calls a "grain beverage," and she wanted me to drink that instead of coffee. Postum's not bad in hot milk if you add enough sugar, but I had trouble staying awake, while she had trouble staying asleep. We needed different cures, it seemed to me.

"What are the worms doing?" I asked.

"Eating," she said.

"Weren't they doing that all day?"

"Yes." She sipped her Postum and leaned forward to point at one of the white creatures. He held his head up and swayed as if he were hearing a wonderful holy voice. "That's called the praying position," she said. "He's waiting to shed his skin and move to the last instar. If you disturb them while they're doing this, they can get stuck or die."

"I thought he was begging for more salad," I said, pretty concerned, suddenly, that I might have disturbed a few praying caterpillars while showing the collection to Greenie or adding mulberry leaves. The white caterpillar waved his strange noggin in the air and swayed like someone who was closing his eyes to shut out the material world.

"What did you and Robby do today?" she asked, her eyes on the mesmerizing caterpillar, not on me.

Discussed Uncle Hoyt's adultery, I almost said because I have a powerful impulse at all times to spill the beans. It's like I'm always under the influence of scopolamine, which, if you haven't watched *The Guns of Navarone* as many times as Robby and I, is the drug the Nazis give the Allied prisoner to make him reveal when the American ships are going to attack. I knew that if my mom kept quizzing me, if she had any inkling of what was going on, I'd end up saying that Hoyt was turning out just like Dad.

"Homework," I finally said.

"Is that all?"

"Uh-huh."

I listened to the caterpillars that weren't ready for their last instar and then for something bigger out in the grove—an owl, say, or some coyotes. Coyotes make the worst demonic chorus you've ever heard when they're closing in on some animal they've cornered—a house cat or a baby rabbit or a possum or somebody's helpless lapdog. Right after we moved into this cottage, I opened the door to go to school and nearly stepped right in the mess of innards that a coyote left on the doormat: the liver, stomach, colon, and—grossest of all—severed head of a rat. Not even Robby would bury it for me. "If we were living in eastern Transylvania," he said, "this would be an omen."

I couldn't hear an owl or any coyotes, though, just the caterpillars unsticking their sticky feet.

"Shouldn't you go back to bed now?" I asked my mother.

"Pretty soon," she said. The mug of Postum sat cold on her lap as she stared at the meditating caterpillar.

"Maybe you should get a puppy," I said, afraid that she was getting too attached to creatures with what seemed to me a fairly high incidence of accidental death.

"Night, Pearl," she said, and went on with her vigil.

ELeven

My father hadn't called me for a month. He sent little e-mails about loving me and missing me and hoping we could work through this, but when I didn't respond, he gave up. It bothered me that he gave up so easily, and then one morning I opened the mail.

"Mom?" I said. "This says our health insurance has been canceled. Can that be right?"

My mother was sitting on our porch with my uncle Hoyt, eating mulberries from a bowl. "Let me see that," my mother said, and her face tightened so that the two lines between her eyebrows nearly met.

My uncle took the notice from her and found a pair of reading glasses in his pocket. He unfolded them and started to read.

"What happened?" I asked.

"Why didn't you tell me?" Hoyt asked my mother. "I could have paid it."

"The bill doesn't come to me," my mother said. "It goes to Glen in Phoenix."

"Why didn't he pay it?" I asked.

"He didn't pay it," my mother said in a trembling angry voice that made her spit out each word like the seed of an especially bitter lemon, "because he's a selfish, cowardly—" She stopped. I knew the psychiatrist had asked her to refrain from criticizing my father in front of me.

"I think the word you're looking for, Sharon," my uncle said, folding the bill decisively and sticking it into his shirt pocket, "is spineless son of a bitch." No one ate any more mulberries after that. Hoyt stood up and went home.

The weather had turned gloomy, too. The blue skies of April are followed by what locals call Gray May, which to me sounds like this cranky, complaining girl you want to slap because she's such a whiner. One good thing had happened, though. A few days later, Hoyt told me that Esteban, the grove manager, hadn't found anything bad to say about Amiel, and Amiel could come every Friday.

"Thank you," I said.

"Nothing to thank me for," he said. "I'll have to let him go if he doesn't work out. The talking thing might be a problem over time. If they don't get to trust him."

"Oh," I said, worried again.

I decided that if I wrote Amiel a note, maybe I could learn more about him and pass this information on somehow. This assumed Amiel could even read the Spanish I put together like a blind person arranging colors.

Juggle = hacer malabares; engañar; trampar
Engañar = to deceive
Trampar = to trick

I arranged and rearranged the words until finally, on a gray misty Friday morning before school, I stood on the driveway, a folded note in my sweaty hand, and I hoped it said:

> *What is your favorite food?*
> *Where did you learn to juggle?*
> *Would you please tell me how you lost your voice?*

While I was standing there, my cell phone startled me, and I found myself staring at my father's name on the screen: GLEN DEWITT.

I ran my fingers over the edge of the paper and watched the foggy edges of the grove. I listened for the whir of Amiel's bicycle, and the phone rang again, then again, until I finally said a grudging hello to my father.

"Pearly girl!" my father said. I could imagine him wearing a perfectly starched pink shirt. Cuff links. Obsession for Men cologne.

"Where are you?" I asked.

"The office," he said. "You ready for a surprise?"

"I don't know," I said. A surprise could be dinner at which he would introduce me to the woman or man who must have been eating with him for all those months at La Vache and the French Laundry while he was so-called missing us.

"This is a pretty damn good surprise," he said. "It's a place."

The purple jacaranda tree was blooming its head off where I stood. Jacarandas can make the whole world look like a Technicolor dreamland, as if Walt Disney had decided everything green should be purple.

"Just think of the place you've always wanted to go," my father said, waving his own Technicolor wand.

I pictured, because I couldn't help it, the Eiffel Tower. Every August, Agnès, Robby, and Hoyt went to Paris to visit her mother, and although they had twice invited me to go with them, both times my parents had come up with reasons why the timing was bad.

I watched the dirt road where Amiel still wasn't riding in on his bicycle, and I touched the folded note that I hoped said, *Where did you learn to juggle?* not, *Where did you learn to deceive?*

"Well, what are you thinking?" my father asked.

"I don't know," I said, because I couldn't tell him about Amiel and I didn't know how to ask why he had canceled our health insurance.

"Paris, France," my father said to me from what felt like a faraway room. "This summer. I know someone who actually has a pied-à-terre in Paris, France, so you just need to tell me when you're going to be finished with school, and I mean finished with the learning part—no need to stay for those days when everyone's just signing yearbooks and flirting around. . . ."

I had an inkling about who owned the pied-à-terre, though I didn't know if the someone was male or female, and I wondered what my dad thought my mother would do with herself while I was in Paris, France, with him and his mistress/mistredo. Maybe she would try to move into the fifth instar for human beings, which is I don't know what.

"I have to go, Dad," I said.

"Well, think about it," he said.

"Okay."

I pushed the End button as Amiel's bicycle came humming through the iron arch. He saw me, lifted his fingers in a small wave, and coasted to a stop.

For a second, I couldn't move or breathe. What is it about a person that makes him harmless to others and fatal to you, like a bee sting or a trace of peanut butter? I put the phone in my pocket and took out my folded message, but Amiel was already walking away to the grove, swinging the long metal prong he used to turn the sprinklers on.

"Amiel?" I said. I tried to say the name nicely, with Spanish vowels.

Amiel turned, so he wasn't deaf, just like he said. I held out the piece of paper and he got a worried look. He glanced up at the house, and he turned the sprinkler key slowly in his hand like a baton.

"It's nothing bad," I said.

He took the paper and set the key down so he could unfold it. His shirt was a white and brown plaid, I remember, and I saw for the first time a sort of leather-thong necklace he wore around his neck. I'm not a fan of man jewelry, but this was man jewelry on Amiel's neck, so I studied the disk of black stone lying warm on the soft spot between his collar bones and shivered again. I must have breathed in and out, though I'm not sure how. Amiel read the note or seemed to read it, and he looked up at Hoyt's house again. He neither nodded nor shook his head at me while the purple jacaranda leaves remained supernaturally purple and the fog closed everything in. Amiel put the paper in his pocket and made the sign I had seen him make earlier, his hand in the shape of the letter C.

"¿Sí?" I asked, and he nodded. Before I could figure out what it meant to say "yes" in this situation, he had walked away.

Twelve

"What were you and Marcel Marceau *le* signing about?" Robby asked while we waited in the car for my mother to find her phone in the guesthouse and drive us to school.

"Were you camped out in the xylosma hedge again, Mr. Double-oh-seven?" I asked.

Robby just tapped on his backpack with his wide, flat fingers. I didn't know why we were so rude to each other now. We'd been really good friends our whole lives, and now that I lived in his guesthouse, we sounded like Greenie Coombs and her brother, who bickered twenty-four hours a day.

"Who's Marsell Marso, anyhow?" I decided to ask, hoping that would be non-hostile.

"You don't know who *Marcel Marceau* is? Marceau was a French actor," he deigned to tell me. "A hugely famous mime.

That's why I thought you'd know. Being so mime-freaked and all."

There are times when being good-looking and intelligent make up for sarcasm and bitterness, but this was not one of those times.

"Amiel's not just a mime," I said. "He juggles."

"It's not his choice of self-expression that I'm worried about," Robby said. "You probably shouldn't flirt with him."

"I wasn't flirting! I don't see why I can't talk to someone who has a job here. Your dad's friendly."

"That's different."

"No, it isn't," I said, though I knew it was.

"Can he mime hanging himself?" Robby asked as my mother hurried toward the car holding her coffee cup.

She opened the car door as I said, "Just stop it."

"Stop what?" she asked.

"Nothing," I said.

It didn't feel like I was headed toward any good discoveries, but I was. I was headed, though I didn't know it, for the river.

Thirteen

By the start of second period, the foggy haze had started to burn off. I wanted to sit in the sun and read or just look at the newly visible turquoise sky and not think about my father or what my note would do to Amiel, but this was school, so Greenie and I just kept shambling toward the redbrick bunker where we had drama with Ms. Grant.

Greenie Coombs became my best friend the last summer of making things up. We were in fourth grade, way too old for playing with Barbies, which is why we were so close: we had to protect our secret. We wanted to give Barbie and Ken a wedding—not just a wedding, actually, but a rehearsal dinner, ceremony, reception, and honeymoon. It was very involved. We found a birdhouse that looked like a chapel at a garage sale and spent five whole dollars on it. We made breath of heaven flower arrangements for the tiny dinner tables and a purple lantana bridal bouquet and a redwood Lincoln Log reception hall and satin dresses for the whole bridal party. Greenie was good at turning one thing into another—at seeing how an acorn cap could be a goblet—and I was good at sewing and believing. Thinking back, it feels like the last time, before Amiel, that I was happy.

Greenie had a pretty face even then, but she was heavy around the middle and her thighs rubbed together. Her hair was black and straight, like a horse's. Her skin was olive and her eyes were green, which was why her brother had given her the nickname. She breathed with her mouth open, which even I could see made her look dim-witted, though she wasn't, not at all. She was good at math, like Robby, so she didn't mind my being good at book reports and vocabulary tests.

Everything was perfect until eighth grade. Greenie was an early bloomer, and while I stayed the same shape, skinny as a tree that grew straight up, the layer of fat around Greenie's middle seemed to move up to her breasts. She got her braces off and started keeping her mouth closed. Then her legs stretched and became thin. By the end of the year, the sort of boys who didn't do their homework began to hover around her locker, never the least interested in me. We stayed friends mostly because Greenie and I had this history together, our secret power to bring inanimate things to life.

I remember that we drifted into second-period drama class that day without interest, though it was our favorite class and Ms. Grant our favorite teacher. The room was always cold because the floor was glossy white concrete and the walls were brick. We were supposed to be brainstorming for a one-act, five-minute play, and as usual Greenie and I were partners. Ms. Grant left the class unsupervised, as she sometimes did, and went into her office while fifteen or twenty of us lay sprawled on the various pieces of furniture that had been donated for stage props. I spent some time at the bookshelves where Ms. Grant ran a lending library of British theater productions and foreign films, looking for something that featured Marcel Marceau. A big droopy guy named Hal told me I should watch *Les Enfants du Paradis*, which turned out not to feature Marcel Marceau at all, but was directed by Marcel *Carné* and featured a totally different famous French mime. I signed it out and put it in my backpack, and while I was throwing out lame ideas for the plot of our one-act, five-minute play, Greenie started in a very low breathy voice to tell me about her upcoming date with this boy named Hickey.

"You're kidding, right?" I said.

"You know that guy who drives a Honda with Texas plates?" she asked, ignoring my attempt to laugh at her boy love's name.

I didn't, but right then Ms. Grant came out of her office and shouted, "I hope from the noise level in this room that you're all going to be ready to write a rough draft of your script in fifteen minutes, including but not limited to Ms. Coombs and Ms. DeWitt?"

So that was all I knew when I was introduced at lunch to a boy I would frankly have called unworthy of breathy-voiced description. His eyes had a sleepy look I associate with low achievement, like most of the boys who were mesmerized by Greenie's breasts. The cuffs of his jeans had come unraveled from dragging along under the heels of his sneakers. His hair hit his eyes mid-iris. He looked older than us, too, which I realized halfway through the conversation was because he had an actual and pressing need to shave.

We were wandering over to the pizza stand when I opened my wallet and saw nothing in there except an old raffle ticket.

"Wait," I said. "I forgot to get money. I'll have to go find my mom."

"You bring your mom to school?" Hickey said.

"Her mother *teaches* here," Greenie told him. "Sometimes. She's a substitute. Mrs. DeWitt."

"Oh, her," Hickey said. I waited for further observations, but he kept them to himself, which made me feel subtly insulted.

"So I guess I'll see you later," I said.

"We could do Pedro's," Hickey said. "I've got, like, this gift certificate."

Fallbrook High doesn't have an open campus, so I said, "But we're not allowed to do that"—the sort of nerdy remark I'd been making since the age of about four.

"Hickey is," Greenie said. "He's eighteen, so he's got a pass."

"He does, but we don't." This, too, is the sort of thing I've been pointing out since the age of four. But Greenie just gave me a pained look, so I followed her to Hickey's car, and nobody saw us.

The taco stand was maybe five minutes away, right on Main Street, an old white cube of a building that my mom says was a *darling* little hamburger and ice cream stand back when Fallbrook was more like downtown Disney. It was my favorite place to eat, and I always ordered the shrimp burrito and horchata, a yummy milk and cinnamon drink. "I'll pay you back," I told Hickey after we shouted our orders in the general direction of the outdoor menu.

"No need," he said. His arms were freckled, and he jiggled the gearshift slightly as we idled at the drive-up window, watching a Hispanic woman fold a tortilla like you'd wrap a newborn baby.

"Let's go eat at the river," Greenie said as soon as Hickey handed over his gift certificate and took three paper bags.

"There isn't time," I said immediately.

"We only have two classes after lunch," Greenie said back, un-Greenie-like.

There was a truck full of construction workers behind us now, waiting with hostile expressions. "Right or left?" Hickey asked.

Left was back to art class and the return to compliance, provided nobody asked us what we were doing off campus.

Right was the river. Sun glinted on the hood of Hickey's car.

"Right!" Greenie said gleefully, and without asking for my vote, her Hickeyman turned right, speeding us past the fake

Irish pub, the Art and Cultural Center, the Mission Theater, the Mexican market, the stoplight, and the brown stucco apartments with sheets draped over the windows.

"You recall that my mother is a sub, right?" I said. "I'm going to get in gigantic, life-threatening trouble, Greenie. So are you, if you care."

"We'll be back before the end of school," Greenie said. "Relax, you big stress cow. You love the river!"

"But I'll be marked absent in art. They'll notice right away what's happened."

"I worked as an aide in the attendance office last semester," Greenie said, poking her straw decisively into her horchata. "They aren't always totally on the ball, I promise. And you know who happens to be working as an aide this period?" She gave me a look I didn't find at all comforting. "Paula Menard. Who totally owes me one."

I adjusted to the situation the way I suppose people adjust to being on a hijacked plane. "So, Hickey," I said, feeling miserable and a little sick. "What's up with the name?"

"You'd have to ask my great-great-granddaddy, I guess." He shifted into gear and went faster than any intelligent person would drive on the tight sunlit curves. Huge oak and sycamore trees grow beside the road to De Luz, and the gullies are full of wild cucumber leaves. It was like traveling, much too quickly, down the green-glass tube of a waterslide.

"Hickey's his last name, dummy," Greenie said with what I guess was an affectionate tone. Her loyalty was with Hickey now. I could feel it.

"What's your first name, then?" I asked, clutching the seats on every curve.

"You won't believe it," Greenie said, delighted with what she knew and I didn't. She sucked horchata through her straw. "Try to guess his name."

"Rumpelstiltskin."

"Ha, ha. Guess again."

"How am I going to guess his name?" I had gone from being panicked about missing school to being annoyed at how tightly I had to clutch the back of Greenie's seat.

"It starts with O," Greenie said.

"Ollie. Oral."

"Oral Hickey! That would be hysterical! But no," Greenie said. "Three wrong, none right."

I was stumped, also carsick. I couldn't think of any other O names. Mr. Hickey downshifted with one freckled arm to take the right fork to De Luz. We were less than a mile from the trailhead if we didn't die in a fiery crash.

"What if a police officer sees us out here on a school day?" I couldn't help asking. "Won't they know we're truant?"

"Truant," Hickey repeated in a slightly mocking voice. Hooted, actually. "Where I come from, we just call it 'ditching.' "

"Guess his name," Greenie urged me. Her perfectly brown, perfectly smooth legs were pressed together underneath her denim miniskirt, which, like most things that Greenie wore nowadays, was millimeters from a dress code violation.

"Ohm," I said.

"Now you're not even saying names. Four wrong, none

right." She paused theatrically, then couldn't wait anymore. "It's *Ormand*," Greenie said, dragging it out for full appreciation. "Isn't that the closest you've ever come, in the flesh, to that guy who's maybe a man, maybe a woman—Orlando?"

Ms. Grant was a big Virginia Woolf fan.

"Watch the comparisons to the half-women types," Hickey said, though he didn't sound that annoyed. He was flying into the dirt parking lot, sending up beige plumes and sprays of white gravel. A big middle-aged guy in a baseball cap was removing the harness from his horse beside a dust-streaked trailer, and I could tell he was making a mental note of the rules we were breaking. When Hickey and Greenie got out of the car, they didn't walk toward the trail I always took with Robby, which was through a yellow stile about twenty yards from the car. Instead, Hickey pushed his burrito into a little white cooler that had been sitting beside my feet the whole time and headed with Greenie toward the road, which they then started to cross.

"Where're you going?" I called.

"There's a swimming hole over on this side," she yelled back. "Hickey showed me."

Except for the horse owner we were alone out there. The hills were covered with purple wildflowers and the green shrubs I didn't know the names of then but can now rattle off like a rosary. The willows in the riverbed were doing that thing I loved, releasing their downy seeds like sideways floating snow. Greenie didn't slow down but kept right on crossing the street, one hand entwined with Ormand Hickey's.

I didn't have a plan, so I followed. I slogged after them through deep sand and powdery dust and oak shade to a steep, crumbling bank where a creek joined the river and made a near U-turn. The water was deep but opaque and khaki-colored in the shade, sky blue in the sun. Reeds clogged the currents that flowed away from us and disappeared around another sharp bend. I felt like I'd reached a foreign river, one where I wouldn't be able to find my way.

Greenie and Hickey kicked their shoes off and sat down in the warm sunshine, and that's when I learned that what Hickey was carrying in his square white cooler was not just his Pedro's burrito but a six-pack of Budweiser. Cold. Pre-purchased. Ready for the not-spontaneous spontaneous outing. I tried to get Greenie's eyes on mine when he snapped a beer out of its plastic bracelet and handed it to her, but Greenie didn't meet my eyes as she casually popped the metal tab. She took a sip, screwed the bottom of the can into the sand so it wouldn't tip over, and began to unwrap her taco like we were all still in Normal World.

I heard the swish of a car on the road. The breeze was soft and sweet-smelling, neither too hot nor too cold. I took out my burrito and though I'm not proud of it, I ate with my usual gusto. The sauce dripped like it always did into the folds of my hands, and like always I didn't have quite enough napkins to get clean. I sucked down in a few gulps the cold, sweet hor-chata. It was like if I finished the food, I could go back and nothing bad would happen. No one would know.

But I finished, and we were still there. My shoes sank into white sand by the khaki water. I balled up the foil wrapping and stuffed it into the paper bag, which I then shoved into my backpack. I tried walking in the direction of the current, and for a minute the glittery water had its old charm. Nubby tadpoles flitted away from my shadow and bright green moss trailed like hair from a piece of driftwood, but when I tried to follow the river around the next curve, I could go barely fifty yards. There was no trail on this side, just reeds and bleached piles of sand and trash—more trash than I'd ever seen on what I considered the real river. The reeds trapped cups, plastic bottles, broken glass, McDonald's wrappers, straws, beer cans, bottle caps, and cigarette stubs. A diaper had been folded into a bundle and left on a shoal like artificial pastry. It disgusted me enough to make me walk back to where Hickey and Greenie were holding hands.

"So what's up with your eyes?" Hickey asked, looking right into them. I was aware this was how I'd framed the question about his name a few minutes ago, so I shouldn't have been offended, but I was.

"I have magic powers," I said.

"Really? What kind?" He flipped his head the way you have to if your bangs are always in your eyes.

"One eye's normal," I said. "It sees the present. The other eye sees the future."

"Cool," he said, humoring me. He took a drink of beer, leaned back on the sand, and asked, "Which is which?"

"Blue sees you here, brown sees where you're going to wind up."

He didn't look amused anymore. He could tell I was being snotty.

"In case you're wondering what you see in the background of that future shot," he said, "the yacht called *I Told You So* is mine."

Hickey had clearly been spending too much time reading the poster in Mr. Fresno's room that showed the rewards of a higher education as a mansion with a Ferrari parked out front.

"Good," I said. "I think I'll take a little walk on the other trail if you guys don't mind. The river's nicer over there."

"Don't you want to fish?" Greenie asked, a little too incredulously, I thought, considering we'd never, ever gone fishing together. "Hickey has a net in the car!"

"Nah, I feel like walking," I said.

"Suit yourself," Greenie said, her sunglasses obscuring her eyes.

I darted back up the bank, through the sand, and across the road, past Hickey's car, past the tire tracks left behind when the horse trailer was pulled away, over the yellow stile thingy, and along the narrow, shadowy, unlittered path, which on this side was overhung with oak and willow and white-limbed sycamore. Tiny flowers bobbed slightly in the breeze. Dragonflies the color of blood hovered and then zoomed away in the direction of water. I could hear the river now like a giant draining bathtub. The farther I went from Greenie and her strange new boyfriend, the better I felt, so I ran for a while. I ran until the path took a sharp turn up into some boulders and I picked my way, goatlike, to the next part of the trail, glad that I had no textbooks in my backpack to weigh me down. Huge trees lay where they had fallen, and a lone duck floated on the water.

I reached the place where I normally left the shady trail for the open sun of the water and found a boulder to sit on. I wanted to do this for a good hour, possibly the rest of my life. I had to think, though, of what Greenie and Hickey would do when they'd finished drinking those beers. Would they start swimming? Necking and fabricating? (If you ask a computer to tell you the French translation for "making love," you get *"fabrication de l'amour,"* which is what Robby and I had called sex ever since: *fabricating.*)

Or maybe Hickey and Greenie would just go back to school and leave me here, unless Greenie made him walk with her along the trail, calling for me like I was a lost dog until Greenie started to worry that I'd been picked up by a serial killer, so she would call the police and give a description of my yellow hooded sweatshirt, my hoop earrings, and my jeans.

At the same moment that I decided to call Greenie and tell her I would just walk all the way home along the river, something I'd wanted to try for a long time anyway, my phone rang inside my yellow pocket. I looked at it first, afraid it was my father again or my mother standing in the attendance office, her face red with the humiliation of having a delinquent child, but it was Greenie.

"Done walking?" she asked.

"No," I said. "Done drinking?" I shouldn't have said anything. That's the way it is with friends and family. If you insist on criticizing them, they want to get rid of you.

"It was just one beer, Miss Priss. I told Hickey we ought to head back, anyway. Get there while Paula Menard can still slip us a tardy pass. Otherwise we'll have to go to Thursday school. Or Saturday school. Or maybe even Sunday school."

"Yeah," I said.

"Meet you at the car, okay?"

"Okay," I said, but it came to me that I could stay there in the sunshine, on a rock, on the river, without Greenie or Hickey or anyone to disturb me. I knew my mother had told all of my teachers that my father had left. She'd made a point of it after I flunked a chemistry test. "Why did you have to tell everybody?" I asked at the time. But now I saw that I had a get-out-of-jail-free card. If I explained that my father had called and invited me to his love nest in Paris, my mother would write me an excuse note, I was pretty sure, and I was also sure my teachers would accept it.

"You know what?" I said to Greenie. "I think I'm just going to stay."

"What?"

"I need to think about some stuff. My dad called."

"Why didn't you tell me?"

"I don't know."

"Okay," she said. "But call me later. I don't want to worry that a mountain lion is digesting you."

I told her I'd call. Then I dialed my mother's cell phone,

which I knew she turned off during the day so it wouldn't ring during her classes, and I left a message about being fine, just being on a walk, working some things out that Dad said that morning, and I'd talk to her later. Then I did something I almost never do outside of school: I turned my phone off.

Fourteen

I stood in the river up to my knees and let the water flow soft and cold around me until I felt, for just a second, that I was moving and the water was still. Then I put my shoes back on and hiked farther along the trail than I'd ever gone and I could see no one, no houses, no power lines, even. Suddenly I was in the wilderness instead of five miles from home. I stopped to breathe a little and looked across the river, where instead of reeds and willow bushes a thicket of oaks and sycamores grew.

The Santa Margarita isn't very deep or fast, so it was strange that I'd never explored the other side. Mostly the other side didn't look that interesting, but these trees were tall and elegant and protective. I looked down at the river and decided it wasn't too deep, that I could probably walk across if I rolled my jeans up high enough and used a few rocks as stepping-stones. I ended up soaking my thighs, but it was worth it: under the oaks it was foresty and dark and spacious. It was so peaceful and level that you could have pitched a tent, and as I walked around thinking about that, I realized that two sycamores in the farthest corner had an actual, genuine hammock tied to them. Not the big ropy kind but the type made of green string that looks like it'd barely hold a bunch of apples.

"Hello?" I said.

Nobody answered. I set my backpack on the ground and spread the strings apart, lost my nerve, and looked around. Who would care, really, if I lay down in an empty hammock? No one or, possibly, the owner.

I listened to a pair of woodpeckers tapping on opposite sides of the river. DOT DOT DASH DOT, one went. DOT DOT, went the other.

Then I just did it. I pulled apart the hammock strings and scrunched in. It was very, very comfortable once I was banana-shaped, and the longer I lay there, the sleepier I got, the more sense the woodpeckers made, and the less I worried about who owned the hammock.

Had this been *Sleeping Beauty*, Amiel would have kissed me. Had it been a slasher movie, I would have awakened to the snapping of a twig. But when my eyes flipped open, the foresty grotto was just quiet: wind ruffling leaves and water tumbling over rocks and a hawk way up in the blue. I unpeeled myself from the hammock and slumped into my backpack.

I had no idea how much farther I had to walk. I passed under bowers strung with wild cucumber, more oaks and sycamores, and the river got smaller and smaller until it was a tiny creek. The trail led away from the creek into a dry meadow and then to a matching yellow stile and Land Conservancy sign. I had reached the end of the trail and the dead end of Willow Glen Road, which meant I had a long way to go, most of it uphill.

I heard a bicycle, and because sometimes the world gives you what you want, the bicycle that streaked into view held Amiel. He slowed down and I stayed hidden in the shade of a big broken tree. He circled once where the asphalt came to an end, then circled again, and then he hoisted his feet gracefully onto the seat of the bicycle. Once his two feet were poised on the seat, he slowly extended one leg behind him, and then he stood up for one breathless second, gliding away from me with one hand on the handlebar, the other straight up. He brought his leg and hand back down until he was seated again and, after pedaling to renew his speed, tipped both feet back behind him until he was lying flat on the bicycle. He lay very straight, like Superman in flight, and then he arranged himself normally on the bike and headed straight for where I stood.

I don't see how it helps the reproductive process to be dumb in the presence of potential mates, unless this is one of those leftover primitive responses that made cavewomen easier to subdue.

I think I said, *"Hola."*

He looked startled.

"That was great," I said. "You're really good."

He nodded slightly and held on to his bicycle. I tried to think how to ask where he lived. *"¿Dónde?"* I said. *"¿Su casa?"*

and he waved his hand to the north. I looked up at the hills and saw avocado groves, a white house, a brown house, and a shed, all of them far apart and none of them connected by driveways to where we stood.

"I've been walking," I said, wishing I knew more Spanish. I did a little head toss to indicate the trail. I was disconcerted by his slender fingers, his bare arms, the flattish angle of his brown cheeks. "I've hiked really far, in fact. The bicycle's a much better way to get around."

He nodded and watched me with his sepia eyes.

"I've got to walk all the way home, too," I said. *"Caminar."* More of the universal finger-walking signal and head bobbing, this time in the direction he'd come from.

For some reason, he smiled and I saw that he had teeth like dental masonry, very white and square. He looked back up the first steep hill of Willow Glen and nodded. I was hoping he'd say something to me, though I'd never heard him speak. He reached into his pocket then and pulled out a small piece of paper that was the same piece of paper I'd handed him in the morning. I took the paper from him, and before I could read it, he was doing that casual ride-off move I have never managed on my own bicycle, where you coast a bit on the pedal before swinging your leg over the bar.

"Gracias," I said.

He turned his head slightly, waved, and kept riding slowly in the direction of a dirt road that curved away from the trail and around an aloe field. I still couldn't see how that road would lead toward the houses north of us, but I was desperate to read his note, which for a while made walking up Willow Glen feel like floating:

Below the question that I hoped was *What is your favorite food?* he'd written in a curiously foreign printing, *cangrejos*.

After *Where did you learn to juggle?* he'd just written, *México*.

How did you lose your voice? was followed by: *Tuve un accidente.*

What kind of accident? In a car? For at least five minutes the fact that he'd written back to me at all kept my mind off the walk, but the road went on and on and up and up. Like most roads in Fallbrook, it led mostly to no-trespassing signs and electric gates and watchful dogs and fruit trees. I gave up hope of walking all the way home and turned on my little black phone, which held four increasingly irate messages from my mother. When I called her, she said she'd pick me up so that she could personally kill me. I said those were terms I could accept.

After all, I had in my pocket a conversation with Amiel.

Fifteen

Cangrejo means "crab," my Spanish dictionary informed me. I would eagerly and promptly have told Amiel how much I, too, like crabmeat, but I had no way to reach him and I was grounded. My mother didn't find my father's phone call much of an excuse, as it turned out. The second I got in the car, she said, "Where did I go this morning?"

"The high school."

"And the day before that?"

I wasn't positive where she'd been subbing the day before. "Potter?" I said.

"And the day before that?"

"I don't remember, Mom. I don't remember every school you went to in the past week."

"Work," she said. "I went to *work*. I didn't go to the river

71

or the mall or the movies or the beach because I was depressed and didn't want to face people."

"Okay."

For cutting school and not answering my phone and wandering loose among mountain lions and would-be rapists ("did you know there are *squatters* camps out there?" my mother asked, so I didn't mention the hammock), she grounded me and took away my phone. The next morning, she refused to make Icelandic pancakes, which were the sacred centerpiece of our Saturday mornings.

"Tell Robby I said *joyeux anniversaire*," I told my mother when the catering trucks began to arrive at ten, filling Hoyt's driveway and the patio with white-shirted men and women. My aunt Agnès was throwing a party for Robby's seventeenth birthday, and I could hear her voice as she told people where to set up chairs and where to chill the Perrier.

My mother appeared to be thinking it over. "You can go to the party," she said, "because I'll be there."

I hoped hopelessly that my uncle might have hired Amiel to do some of the work. "Okay," I said. "Thanks."

My mother and I walked through the grove in our new summer dresses, my mother's hair pulled into a bun, her mouth similarly tightened, at six. We braced ourselves because a party thrown by Agnès was so elegant that you could only enjoy it if you were, say, invisible and yet able to eat. I was always charmed, at first, by the food and the flowers and the little sparkling lights, her handsomeness, and the waiters with trays. Agnès stood at the far edge of the patio, holding a champagne flute, her dark hair curling up just a little at the back of her ageless neck. I saw immediately that the summer dresses my mother and I had chosen were frowsy and countrified and that we would always and forever be that kind of people. Agnès had that effect on me. The evening sky was periwinkle, and white roses glowed at the edges of a world that smelled of grilled meat and caramelized sugar, where heaps of impossibly perfect strawberries cascaded over one another on silver platters and arrangements of incandescent lilies floated in the center of each round table. The pool water flowed over its vanishing edge, one I had approached from within too many times to be taken in by the illusion.

I doubted Robby was very pleased with the offering. For my fifteenth birthday, my mother, father, Robby, and I had driven to Oceanside and walked the length of the old wooden pier to Ruby's Diner, where the red and white booths seem to float over the water in a shimmering light that's the best part of winter in San Diego. The ocean below our windows was mint blue while we were twisting our straw papers and sucking chocolate milk shakes out of tall fluted glasses, and my father was in a cheerful mood because he'd just sold a condo, I think. Then one of the men leaning over the rail with a fishing rod just outside our window caught a bat ray. I remember that part because when we walked out of the restaurant and stood looking out at the hammered pools of silver light where the late sun touched down, Robby asked what the point was of killing a bat ray.

The woman who sat with the dead ray at her feet said, "Have you ever eaten scallops, kid?"

"Yeah," Robby said.

"Then you've probably eaten a ray. Restaurants cut them with a cookie cutter, see, and call them scallops."

I didn't believe her at first, but Robby did.

"That doesn't happen," I said when we walked away.

"I'll bet it does," Robby said.

"I don't see what difference it makes," my father said when we were all strolling down the pier past the fishing rods and tubs of bait and men standing with their hands in their coat pockets, waiting for a catch in the cold, late-evening wind. "You're eating something that used to be alive, one way or the other."

"But you cut it up and leave all those extra bits," I said, "and those parts go to waste." The cookie cutter thing reminded me of making sugar cookie trees at Christmas and trying really hard to use up all the dough, though you never could.

"Plus, they're lying," my mom said. "They're saying it's something it isn't. That's the main thing."

"I wonder what they make shrimp out of," Robby said. "Sharks?" He was joking, trying to turn the conversation away from morals. "Hey, check that guy out."

Beyond the fishing lines, a V of black-suited surfers bobbed up and down on their boards, eyes on the next swell, hoping to eke out one more ride before total darkness. The boy Robby pointed to had just risen, and he stood in perfect balance as the wave held him and carried him for a long beautiful time, and when the boy saw that the ride was over, he stepped off the board.

Looking at Robby beside the tea lights and the swimming pool, his pants tailored and his shirt pressed, I thought he looked like someone who could ride a long way without falling off.

"Shoot me now," he told us, giving my mother a hug.

"Not when you're looking so princely," she said, full of her usual love for him. She handed over the box that I knew contained a small statue of a red-kilted Tintin and his terrier, Snowy, standing in a rowboat as they prepared, according to the catalog description, to set off for L'Ile Noir.

"Thanks," Robby said, and before I could say anything more, my uncle was there, smooshing me pleasantly to his granite chest, his face cut a little from shaving or crashing through bushes on his motorbike.

"Come eat," Hoyt said. "Agnès brought you some of those chocolates, Sharon Magoo. From Par-ee. Plus we have scallops wrapped in bacon."

I raised an eyebrow at Robby.

"Real ones," Robby said. "Or so they promised."

When my uncle walked away with my mother, Robby pulled me back and hissed into my ear, "There's an Avalon in the driveway. I think it's the one, but I couldn't check it out when everybody was still arriving."

"He invited his girlfriend to your party?"

Robby shrugged.

"Why would he do that?"

Robby widened his eyes to show that logic had no place here. "Just come check it out with me," he said, giving me the sweet old Robby look, the one that said I was his best cousin of all. He led me past various neighbors and friends, all of whom he nodded to with what I have to say was his mother's charm, and then dragged me through the darkened wisteria arbor to the gravel drive, which was crowded with cars and trucks that gleamed in the fading light. "There," he said, checking to see that no one was watching or listening to us. He let go of my arm and approached the car as if it were an alien spaceship, which I suppose in a way it was. Stars glittered like moving water overhead.

"Keep watch," he said. He leaned forward to peer through the windows. "It's the same one," he said, "and it's unlocked."

"You're kidding," I said. "Then get in."

"Get in?"

"Nobody's coming. Just get in and find the registration."

Robby climbed into the car and opened the glove compartment. The car's interior lights lit up the whole scene like a fish tank, and at that moment I heard my uncle calling, "Robby?"

I couldn't see where Uncle Hoyt was, exactly. There was a catering truck to one side of us and somebody's Dodge dually on the other side, and though I could see most of the front lawn, I couldn't see my uncle, so I ducked.

The voice came closer.

"Robby?"

The light in the car went out. I had no way of knowing whether Robby had also heard the voice and ducked.

"I don't know where he went," my uncle told somebody. "I'll send him to find you when he shows up, okay?" he said.

I earnestly hoped that might be the end of his search, but then I saw my uncle's silhouette at the far end of the corridor that the parked cars formed on the grass and gravel. He would see me. He would see me crouched beside a car and he'd know whose car it was and what would I say? What if he came up and saw Robby in the front seat?

I popped up and started walking—sprinting, nearly—toward him, not daring to sneak a glance into the Avalon. "Hi, Uncle Hoyt," I said. My voice sounded fake and wobbly, as a nervous, lying voice will. "I was just looking for something."

"You find it?" He studied me with his usual acuteness. That was the thing that gave Uncle Hoyt real substance, the fact that he always looked like he was weighing your moral fitness and expecting the very best you could be, no lies or cowardice, and giving you the same. How could I have been wrong about him?

"Yeah, I found it," I told him, sick at heart. I patted my purse as if the phantom lost thing were safely stowed. I sweated onto the tight batiste armholes of my new unfashionable dress.

"Let's go back to the party, then, okay?" Hoyt said. "Have you seen Robby?"

I said I hadn't lately, and I went with him to the plates of scallops and figs and strawberries and lamb, but I slipped away again from the quivering pool water and the sparkly lights as soon as I could. There in the Avalon was Robby, prone in the dark seat of the car. When he saw me, he cautiously sat up. I opened the car door and discovered that Robby Wallace is not spy material and maybe not, as I thought at the start of the party, the master of his surfboard and the sea.

"Well?" I whispered.

"I don't know. I haven't moved since you left."

"Get cracking, Tintin! I'll be the lookout."

He shook his head, so finally I just did it for him. I got in the car, opened the glove compartment, and rifled away. I told myself it was my father's fault and my uncle's, too, and that I used to be good and trustworthy.

The car was registered to someone named Arnold Farlow on Tumblecreek Lane. I memorized this information and stuffed the papers back into the plasticine folder filled with receipts. I was more than ready to declare this sufficient information when I noticed that there was a laminated tag on the floor of the car—one of those ID cards you have to wear now that people assassinate their co-workers all the time. MARY BETH FARLOW, this one said beneath her photograph, but the interior lights had winked out automatically, so I was trying to make out her face when Robby opened the car door and made all the light I needed. "Someone's coming," he hissed, crouching down on the grass beside the car. "Let's go."

When we returned to the party, my mother said, "I've been looking for you. Stay closer."

Cake was presented, candles were lighted, candles were extinguished, cake was removed from the table by a white-jacketed waiter, and my aunt Agnès said a number of unspecific things about her affection for Robby and Fallbrook and failed, afterward, to include my mother and me in the vast number of guests she invited to step forward and talk into the microphone about Robby. A horse trainer that Robby had always loathed (my aunt Agnès is a big one for horses, Robby not so much) was remembering Robby's first (forced) participation in a dressage show when I looked up to thank the person who was handing me a plate of cake and ice cream and saw that it was Mary Beth Farlow.

She was pretty, of course. Smooth skin, round eyes, swept-up brown hair, a general neatness and smallness and confidence as she handed me a plate and then walked away in her black ballet shoes. I found my uncle in the crowd, but he was not looking at Mary Beth Farlow. I stared hard at Robby, and I waited for him to look back at me. *Her, her, her, her,* I was trying to tell him as the black skirt and white blouse and brown twist of hair weaved in and out of tables, retrieving another plate of cake and melting ice cream, the secret of her tie to the man who was paying for the party hers alone, she supposed, and that was why she glided so neatly everywhere.

"I thank you all for joining us tonight to celebrate *mon petit* Robby, not *petit* so longer," Agnès was saying regretfully, and Robby stood up politely and smiled his gray-eyed smile, which finally landed on me. He read my lips well enough to know I either had something to say or was dying of anaphylactic shock, and after kissing the cheeks of what seemed like fifty guests, he made his way to where I stood like the Grim Reaper. The caterers were swiftly dismantling the bar and hustling the trays of food into the house, and because they didn't always come back out, I had lost track of Mary Beth Fowler.

"What the *le* hell, girl detective," Robby said.

"She *is* here," I hissed.

"Didn't we already know that?"

"She served me a piece of your *le cake*," I said, my eyes on the white shirts passing to and fro, none of them hers.

This made him turn and survey the men and women who were in such a hurry to go home.

"Which one?" he asked.

"She went in the house with a pile of napkins and she didn't come back out."

He strode quickly ahead of me into the house, then remembered he had to let me lead. The kitchen was one of those giant modern spaces composed of granite and steel, and none of the men and women in it stacking trays or washing glasses was Mary Beth. I didn't see my uncle Hoyt, either, although some of his friends sat on oversized leather sofas watching basketball on an oversized television set. Sometimes walking into Robby's house made me feel like I'd climbed a bean stalk into the giant's castle. *Fe, fi, fo, fum.* "And Kobe scores!"

I shook my head to let Robby know I didn't see her, and, worried that my mother would come looking for me, I started for the front door, weaving in and out of neighbors and strangers who turned to say goodbye to Robby. He got nabbed by a group of affectionate elderly women, and by the time I reached the farthest row of cars, there was a meaningful gap where Mary Beth's Avalon had been and a scab of mud where her tires had dug into wet grass.

Robby came up beside me and looked at the car hole. Stars shone above us, and the cold-water smell of the grove, a wet, rocky, pipe-clean odor, rose from the ground.

"What're you going to do now?" Robby asked me, his voice glum. His shirt had come untucked, his tie was loose, and in the darkness I saw that if we were surfers, we were the ones who waited and waited for the right moment, afraid that in our ignorance we would not even know when the right wave was coming or when we should stand.

"I have to go home," I said. "I'm grounded."

"Why? Did your mom find out about Marcel Marceau?"

"There's nothing to find out. I went off campus for lunch with Greenie and skipped the rest of the day."

"Darn," he said. "I was thinking about a swim."

My mother might have let me swim in Robby's pool, but I saw her coming toward us, looking fed up, and I said, "See you, Robby. Happy *le* birthday."

"Yeah," he said. "*Joyeux* good night."

Sixteen

●

The next morning, the air was as cool as rain, the sky spreading its whiteness through the room like a bad headache. Robby woke me by shaking the box of Corn Pops over my head. "*Bonjour le* you. We're going for a drive in my birthday present," he said. "Corn Pops to go?"

"Someone *le* gave you a *car?*" I asked. I didn't make it sound like a good thing. "Please tell me it isn't red."

"It isn't red."

I stood up and went to the window from which, in clear weather, you could glimpse parts of the driveway. I looked suspiciously through the trees.

"It's red," he admitted, looking over my shoulder. "I can't drive it to school, though, until I'm a senior. What kind of sense does that make?"

I didn't answer because I didn't know.

"So where's your mom, anyway?" he asked.

I squinted at a note my mother had left on the coffeemaker:

Went to farmers' market with Louise
because I trust you to observe the rules.
Check out the surprise in the silkworm box!

"Why is there a hairy white egg over here?" Robby asked. He was studying the worm trays with his usual revulsion.

"It's a *cocoon!*" I said in the same voice you might have used to say, "It's a boy!" My mother and I had been waiting for this moment with an embarrassingly high level of anticipation. A few of the worms had reached their fifth instar, which was the last phase of caterpillar fatness, but instead of spinning one strand of silk one mile long into a perfect oval, as we'd been led to expect, they had turned a pale feverish yellow, then saffron, then mahogany brown, and then died feet up in a sad pool of oozing juices. I was surprised my mother hadn't dragged me out of bed to behold the reversal of our fortunes.

I stared at the exquisite white cocoon with maternal pride until Robby said impatiently, "Ready?"

"You know," I told him, "for an honor student you have a remarkable lack of scientific curiosity."

"It's not a lack of scientific curiosity," he said, shaking his head and pouring my Corn Pops for me. "It's an aversion to worms."

I picked through a basket of clean, depressing clothes that no one had managed to fold. We lived basket to basket now that we no longer had to spruce up for my dad. "Where are we going in your fancy red car, anyway?" Clearly, he had forgotten that I was grounded.

"Your favorite place."

Paris? I thought of saying, but the memory of my father's invitation soured the joke.

"*Le* river," Robby said, putting the cereal box away without folding down the liner or closing up the box, a carelessness that was too careless even for us. I resisted the urge to fix the box in front of him. "And one other place," he added.

When I hid in the bathroom to change out of my pajamas and think about what would happen if I went to the river while I was grounded, I shouted out questions about where the other place might be, but he wouldn't say.

"To see your pal Monsieur Ostrich?" I asked in a French accent.

"No."

"To buy me donuts?"

"No."

"So what kind of car is it? Have you named it yet?"

"I'm thinking of 'the Fabricationist,'" he said. By now we were standing on the porch. In front of us was a paper sign my mother had taped to the screen door. It said,

REMEMBER YOU ARE GROUNDED.

"I forgot," Robby said. "You can't go."

"We'll just have to hurry," I said, shoving open the door

and walking through fog and avocado leaves until I stood beside a bright red two-door Honda.

"Are you sure?" he asked.

"Let's go," I said.

As soon as we passed over the freeway and began to skim along the tight curves of Mission Road, I became even more reckless. "You know what," I said. "I could show you a different part of the river. I found a new trail entrance the other day."

"Okay," he said, cheerful about his new car or his intentions or maybe both. He had a little crescent-shaped scar on his cheek that he believed was my fault, though I didn't remember scratching him when I was five. It looked deeper in the foggy light. The road twisted in and out of half-seen oaks, and we spiraled slowly down to the riverbed among the crows and hawks and chittering ground squirrels, but we didn't pass Amiel. We passed no humans at all, in fact. We parked at the place where I'd seen Amiel last, and I stared up at every house that might be his.

We began to hike past the dry meadow, waist high with fennel, and at the top of a hill, Robby stopped to read a Land Conservancy sign I hadn't noticed before. "Agua Prieta Creek this way," Robby said. "Is that where we're headed? Dark Water Creek?"

"Yes," I said, not really sure it was the right way until I saw the arch of oaks and sycamores that led, like a living tunnel, to the river itself. "Yeah, this is right," I said. Just then we caught up to a man, a border collie, and a little boy.

"Look, Dad!" the boy said. "The hobos made a jump for

their bicycle!" and he pointed to a steep, well-packed bump in the trail.

For a while, we could hear him pointing out all the hobo improvements.

"Look! The hobos have a swing!" he said, and that one was obvious: vines hanging down from a cluster of trees. I didn't know what he meant by a hobo pineapple tree until I saw a funny little palm tree, no taller than my knee, with a trunk that was shaped just like a pineapple.

"Hobo traps!" (Metal lockboxes someone dumped under a tree.)

"That's where the hobos keep their alligators." (A stagnant algae-green pond.)

"This is a hobo finder," he announced before they took another path and headed out of our hearing. The boy picked up a forked stick that my mother would have called a water witcher. "They use it to find things," the boy said.

Once we were alone, Robby started pointing to stuff like a tour guide and saying, "Hobo fish farm." "Hobo bathtub." "Hobo slide."

"We should move out here," I said. "The hobos are having all the fun."

Every year on Halloween until I was about eleven, my mother sewed, glued, and/or papier-mâchéd me into some complicated, uncomfortable costume, and then if I complained that it was scratchy and I didn't want to wear it, she would say, "Fine. You can just go as a hobo, like I always was."

"What is a hobo, exactly?" Robby asked.

"What adults used to be for Halloween," I said.

He frowned and took aim at a huge fennel plant, then whacked it with a branch he'd picked up along the way. The trees were green overhead now, and all the color was coming back into the world. "Unless they were French," he said. "I don't think my mother was ever a *le* hobo."

"Why is it that no one ever says he's going to be a homeless person for Halloween?" I asked. "Or an illegal alien?"

"Why can you be a pirate and not a Nazi?" Robby asked, using his branch as a tester for water depth. We were standing on the edge of a nice round virgin pool, green-rimmed and flecked with water skaters. A sun-bleached log formed a picturesque bridge, which Robby began to cross.

We weren't far now, it occurred to me, from the hammock.

"You know what?" I said. "You won't believe the hobo bed I found in here the last time I was hiking."

"Ew," Robby said.

"No," I said. "It was a hammock, not a mattress. I'll show you."

Everything is farther the second time. I led him under countless oaks and over countless anthills, through dappled shade, gnat clouds, and stuff I really hoped wasn't poison ivy. Finally, we stood at the edge of the wide, rippling water, and I sat down to remove my shoes, so Robby obediently did the same, and we went sloshing through cool water under a sky that felt enormous and unspoiled. I led Robby into the grotto and stood before the tree. "Here," I said, but there was no hammock.

"It was right here," I repeated. I touched the trunks of nearby trees, searching for string or string marks.

Robby walked around with an interested look. I wandered behind him, assuring him, as I swatted insects from my face, that I'd taken a nap *right here,* and then I stopped to examine what I thought was a nest. It turned out to be a swirl of dried river algae baked to the color of straw. Robby kept walking, and in a few minutes I heard him say, "Check this out."

He was holding a tin pot in one hand, and with the other he pointed to what I had assumed was a big pile of driftwood. The river was never the same height. Sometimes, the rains fell hard through January and February and the river thundered through here for a month, but it always dried up again, leaving dry islands of uprooted trees and waist-high nests of algae like the one I'd just touched.

I walked closer to where Robby stood, and I realized that the silvery wood wasn't just a random pile. It was sticks laced together to *look* like a random pile. When you walked around the other side, as Robby had done, you saw a crude but clever house. It was barely six feet high—lower in the doorway—and the other three walls were made of wood scraps, tin, and rocks. The best part was a sort of stained glass window made of glass bottles wedged into an old window frame. One bottle was blue and one was brown, but the others were clear and had been arranged like puzzle pieces.

"Isn't this the greatest?" I said. "It's like your tree house, only with *found* stuff. Like a fort you can really live in."

"The hobo really has been living it up out here," Robby said, and I could tell he didn't think it was the greatest. I checked my watch. I knew the farmers' market was a forty-five-minute drive, one way. And Louise was the type to talk to every peach seller and crepe maker. Still, I was nervous.

Robby set the pot down on a counter built of more river stones and some mismatched tiles. He opened another pot and lifted up a bag of tortillas to show me, then pointed to a plastic bag strung from a nail on the wall. It was full of ramen noodle packages, the cheapest food on earth. Robby walked out of the house again, still in full surveillance mode, and I wondered how you cooked ramen noodles here without getting caught. Wouldn't a hiker or a Friend of the Fallbrook Land Conservancy see the smoke?

I didn't like the way Robby casually examined everything, but while he was outside, I did touch one thing: on a little stump of wood beside the blanket was a tin box, an ornate cylinder with fluted sides and black and gold latticework, scabbed with rust, that framed two faded, greenish scenes of courtly dancers. On one side, a man played a lute for a woman perched on a cushion. On the other, they had begun to dance.

I shouldn't have opened the box, but I did, and when I looked inside, I expected to see rolled-up money or change. What I saw in the bottom of the tin, though, just as Robby said, "There are some hobo bicycle tracks out here," was a business card and a photograph. The business card said AMIEL DE LA CRUZ GUERRERO. HARD WORKER. The photograph showed a woman in a gingham smock standing in front of a turquoise wall with a red door half open behind her. Her hair was long and black. She wasn't smiling as she rested both hands on the shoulders of a little boy with a narrow, hopeful face.

"I think we should tell the police," Robby said. His voice was very close to the door, and as if hiding the photograph would be enough to save Amiel, I dropped it and the card back into the tin box, closed the lid, set the box on the stump, and made for the doorway.

"Why?" I said.

"This is obviously some migrant worker's camp, and you can't just live in a nature preserve."

I realized this must be how I sounded to others most of the time. "Why not?" I asked.

"It's a fire hazard, for starters." Robby pointed to the bicycle tracks in a deep pile of white sand. "That's how he gets here."

"We should go," I said. "My mother's going to come home."

Robby looked at his watch, nodded, and picked up his shoes to wade back through the river.

"I think we'd better go right back," I said. I felt the sinking of each bare foot and imagined Amiel studying our tracks. Illogically, I wanted Amiel to know that the tracks were mine. But he wouldn't. It would just scare him to see that two strangers had come into his hiding place, and maybe he would have to disappear now, as the hammock had. Maybe I would return and find nothing but the false nests the river spun for itself in the willows. I let my legs sink into the cold jade-green water and followed Robby to the other bank.

"Where were we going, anyway?" I asked. "I mean the second place."

"Tintin's on the trail," Robby said.

"Whose trail?"

"Mary Beth's, of course."

"I think Tintin better drop me at home," I said.

"Come on," Robby said. "Let's get something to eat first. It won't take that long."

"How long?"

"Thirty minutes."

I practically ran back to his car, and I was still sweating when he pulled the car into the parking lot behind Café Chartreuse.

"Is Tintin paying?" I asked.

"Tintin always pays," Robby said.

Seventeen

She was our waitress, of course.

"*What* the *le* hell are you doing?" I asked Robby when Mary Beth had gone to a far corner of the restaurant.

"Assessing," he said calmly. "It's MBF, isn't it? She's the same height as the woman I saw from the hedge, plus this café did the catering last night."

"Yes," I said. I bit a fingernail too bitten to need work and looked around for friends of my mother's.

Mary Beth came over to ask, "Have you decided?" If she was tired, it didn't show, and if she recognized Robby, she didn't say. I thought she was studying him more intently than she studied me, but that was natural. Robby was good-looking even in his stretched-out T-shirt and old tennis shorts and the shoes that he wore without socks. Greenie used to want me to set her up with him, but Robby was so indifferent when she was around that she finally gave up.

"What's your most irresistible sandwich?" Robby asked, looking adorably curious.

"Statistically speaking," Mary Beth said, "I'd have to say salmon. Though a lot of people order the goat cheese, too. And the Brie."

He acted like she'd said something profound. "The salmon," he said.

Personally, I wondered why Mary Beth was still in Fallbrook. Robby and I were both too ambitious and snobby to consider colleges within commuting distance.

"Do you have crab?" I asked.

"Not for lunch," she said.

I ordered a panini and my mind drifted to Amiel's house. I wondered how many other day laborers lived in the ravines and thickets of Fallbrook and whether we would like them better if we called them hobos. I also wondered what would happen if my mother walked into the café.

When Mary Beth disappeared into the kitchen, Robby asked, "What do you think?"

"Think?"

"Of MBF."

The name had a vaguely insulting air, I suppose because of the F. "She's conventionally pretty," I said.

"You know the owner, right?"

"Sort of." Mr. Eckert was standing at the espresso machine

when we arrived, and I was relieved that he hadn't seemed to notice me. I was dreading the questions he might have about my father, who used to bring me to the café for breakfast on his home weekends and sit at the counter afterward, talking to Mr. Eckert about Italy and New York, two places my father had once thought I ought to see.

"Quiz him a little. Get the *le* scoop."

"But he'll wonder why I'm so nosy."

"So? Come on. Please. You of all people should understand what's at stake here."

I pictured Robby's giant house turning upside down and coming to rest on its giant stone chimney. I pictured the foundation covered with soil and worms and roly-poly bugs as it was exposed, for the first time, to everybody's shameless scrutiny. I won't say that I didn't feel that horrible niggling wish for other people's lives to be as screwed up as my own.

"Please?" he asked again.

"Fine. I'll pry for you. But only if you promise not to tell the police what we saw today," I said. "I mean the hobo house."

Robby tapped his fingers on the table and studied me like my father's divorce lawyer had studied my mother's divorce lawyer. "All right," he said. "I won't tell the feds on El Hobero."

In spite of my work in Ms. Grant's drama class or maybe because of it, I'm a terrible actress, and I began to get nervous when I saw Mr. Eckert heading toward us with tall glasses of pink soda. I asked Robby, "Can I say that I'm asking because you want to know?"

"Sure," Robby said. "I *do* want to know."

"Here you go, Pearl," Mr. Eckert said, setting the drinks down in front of us. "Good to see you again. How's your dad? I haven't seen him for ages."

"Oh," I said. "He moved."

"Moved?"

"Out," I said. I was surprised no one in town had told him. Usually, I heard about affairs and divorces and drug problems that way: from adults talking to each other.

"Then how are *you*?" Mr. Eckert said.

"Oh, fine," I said, grateful to have Robby's life to discuss instead. "Can I ask you a question?"

"Sure."

"It's about your waitress," I whispered. Mary Beth was talking to customers on the other side of the room, but the café wasn't very big.

Mr. Eckert bent forward and looked amiable but concerned.

"You know my cousin, Robby, right? He has a crush. On her, actually. We're doing reconnaissance." I paused for a second because I didn't know how to ask if Mr. Eckert had, by chance, seen Mary Beth with Robby's father. "Is she *single*?" I asked.

"Far as I know."

"What else can you tell us? He needs, you know, a flirting angle."

"Kind of mature for you, isn't she?" Mr. Eckert said to Robby, not entirely disapproving, maybe even impressed. "You're still at the high school, right? Well, let's see. She's studying gerontology. Sophomore year, I think. She lives with her parents, very nice also. Her father's an eye doctor. She had a tennis scholarship to UCLA but pulled something."

I was stuck on the gerontology part. She was training to take care of old people and dating a fifty-year-old man?

Mr. Eckert stopped talking because Mary Beth was coming toward us with our sandwiches. "Mary Beth?" Mr. Eckert said. "Have you met Pearl DeWitt before?" Mary Beth shook her head politely and set my plate in front of me. I could tell she wanted to remain strictly anonymous.

"This is her cousin . . ." Mr. Eckert started to say, waiting for me to fill in the blank, but Robby beat me to it.

"Robby Wallace," he said. "I think you were at my house last night."

Mary Beth gave him his plate with the air of someone who has been lit by a motion detector.

"My *overblown* birthday party," he added.

"Oh, that's where I've seen you," she said, as if she'd just that second figured it out. "Happy sixteenth!" Her hands were free, so she tucked a piece of hair behind her ear. It didn't stay.

"*Seven*teenth," he said.

I really didn't know the script at this point. Mr. Eckert winked at me, mistaking Mary Beth's flustered look for a romantic interest in Robby, and went off to seat a group of people I was glad I didn't recognize.

"So you play college tennis?" he asked Mary Beth.

"I'm not playing right now. I did," she said. Her face was

red from what I guessed was a little internal voice repeating *Oh my God Oh my God*. I felt a little sorry for her, though she didn't really deserve it.

"You don't give lessons or anything, do you?" Robby asked. "I thought my dad was saying that you did."

"Also past tense," she said. "I pulled a hamstring." She looked nervously around the room. "I'd better go take their order," she said, pointing to another table and starting to walk away.

"Hey," Robby said. "Is your dad Dr. Farlow?"

She nodded.

"The ophthalmologist?"

More nodding.

"My dad keeps saying he's going to get his eyes checked. He has this weird mass in the right eye, this—what's it called—*occlusion*."

She blinked.

"I'll tell him I saw you."

"Okay," she said.

"Occlusion?" I said to Robby in his car on the way home.

"It just came to me," he said.

"Do you have a plan, here?"

"A plan?" he said. "Sort of. Not really. As much as anyone, I guess."

Eighteen

We beat my mother to the house by five minutes. By the time she arrived, I was cleaning Lavar's junky old bathroom. After that, she read a book, and I put away wrinkly clothes that hadn't seen a drawer in weeks. I sat down with my science book opened to the periodic table and looked with a kind of hopelessness at the abbreviations of the noble gases. It was when my mind wandered from He to Uuo that I began to hatch my own Robby-style half-baked plan. If I could sneak out of the house once, why not twice?

My mother had been to the farmers' market, but she'd brought nothing home, not even strawberries, so at about six o'clock, we ate a depressing meal of canned tomato soup and quesadillas. I asked, very casually, if I could go do the rest of my homework in Robby's tree house, and she said okay. I packed my books and then my laptop.

"Why are you taking that?" she asked suspiciously.

"English paper," I said.

For a while, I studied. I read "The Emperor of Ice-Cream," found two examples of alliteration, and explained "how they added to the tone." Then, after wondering for some time what it would be like to live in the tree house, all alone, in Mexico or Guatemala, I climbed down, extracted my bicycle from a spidery part of the Wallaces' shed, pushed it along a gravel drive that was well out of my mother's sight, and rode to the river.

I'd never been there so late in the day, when the light was orange and gnats hung in nameless constellations. In certain parts of the woods, the oldest, biggest trees were burnt to charcoal from past fires, but they'd sprouted soft leaves and young white branches. Vines crept up and over them, a hundred feet into the air. I always felt when I reached these huge shrouded rooms that I'd found my way to a foreign country, a secret wilderness into which I could disappear.

Where the river flowed past Amiel's house, I tightened the backpack that held the components of my plan to show him a mime who'd become famous for doing what Amiel could do. I looked around for joggers, hikers, and dogs but saw only gnats, tadpoles, and a wary duck.

I plunged knee deep into the water and slogged across. I could hardly hear the bubbling-babbling current over my pulse. The river seemed colder, my legs wobbled, and the thicket suddenly had a forbidding look. What if Amiel protected himself with a handmade ax? What if he didn't live alone? I blundered toward the silvery lattice of driftwood and stopped to consider what I would do if a completely different illegal immigrant was sitting there with a gun.

Maybe I should call Greenie and hang up so police could trace the origin of my last and final phone call, I thought.

I was just about to do this when I saw a person standing on the branch of a sycamore ten feet away.

It was Amiel.

He wasn't holding an ax, and his feet were bare. He didn't smile when he saw that I'd discovered his hiding place but watched me with what looked like the hope that I would go away. He just stood in the tree and waited. Everything incredibly stupid about my plan—the movie in my backpack, my heavy laptop, the bicycle I would have to ride home in the dark on a winding road afterward—revealed itself.

And yet I blundered on. "I wanted to show you something," I said.

If he understood me, he gave no sign. He didn't nod. He didn't climb down. The sun was at the vanishing point beyond us, a final glimmering orangeness in the west. I looked behind me and saw only reeds—no hikers or joggers or dogs. I knelt on the sand and unzipped the backpack. I removed the computer and set it on my lap. Then I fumbled with cases and buttons until I made the silvery-black images of *Les Enfants du Paradis* move across the screen. I turned on the Spanish subtitles and tilted the screen so that it faced Amiel up in the tree.

The look on Amiel's face was less forbidding now. The sun went out in a single breath and I shivered, the sand already cold against my knees. In the light that was now turquoise, he looked at me and the screen with what might have been curiosity or just acceptance that I wasn't going to disappear. He jumped down from the tree and walked over to me. He didn't say hello in any language. I felt a stroke of fear like I used to feel as a child when I knew I had pushed my father too far. Amiel reached for the computer, closed it, and the pale silver light of the movie went out.

As I sat on the sand with the closed-up theater on my knees, foolish and ashamed, he walked away from me. I wondered where his bicycle was. I wondered if he had cooked and eaten his dinner and if he ever felt safe enough to take off all his clothes and bathe in the river. The world around us was so beautifully blue-green and sharp that such things seemed natural and ideal, better and purer than my life at home. His bare feet sank in the white sand and his shirt glowed a little in the twilight. I knew I needed to hike out while I could still find the path back, but I watched until he disappeared behind the pile of branches that was his wall. He'd gone into his house without speaking to me.

There was nothing to do, really, but put everything away as quickly as possible and run home.

I turned around one last time and saw him watching me. There was enough light to see his face, but not his expression.

"Sorry," I said. Did he want to talk to me but couldn't? Or *shouldn't*, like Robby said? I remembered Robby asking if Amiel could mime hanging himself, and for some reason, I lifted my hand up in a fist like I was holding a noose around my neck, and then I acted like I was hanging myself. I thought Amiel smiled, but it was so dark I couldn't be sure.

I turned around and whacked my way through the reeds until I stood on the tiny beach. I felt an unexpected dread of the slow-moving water, darker now. It was the same shallow current, of course, holding the same shy creatures, but I was afraid. I told myself to be sensible, and I forced one foot into the water, then the other. I sloshed through in a kind of terror until I found myself on the other side. At first I had no need of my flashlight, but the trees formed a tunnel that was darker than the open spaces. I shined the light chaotically on the ground and up nearby trunks and then down again to make sure I could see any spiders that might have suspended their webs across the path. For a while, I made good time among the unfamiliar cracking sounds and spiky shadows. I heard owls and pictured mountain lions. I heard mice and thought coyotes. Somehow I came to the place where I had to walk along a fallen log to cross the water and told myself it was just like the balance beam and that it wasn't quite dark yet, not black dark, and the log bridge was at least a sycamore, so it was white. I shone my flashlight down on the log, started toward it, tripped on the mud bank, and fell. I cried out too loudly and hysterically, I'm sure, for the injury itself. It was just a scrape on my shin and my hand. I heard footsteps behind me and felt hands on my arms, which shot new fear through me before I turned and saw that it was Amiel. He had followed so quietly I hadn't heard him.

"You scared me," I said. I wanted to grab hold of him, but I just sat there. I thought that if I held still, he would leave his hands on my arms, but he didn't. He let go.

He gestured for me to stand up, and I did. I brushed feebly at my dusty shorts and glanced at my shin, which throbbed. There was nothing impressive about the scrape, unfortunately. I could see only a needle-fine slash of blood in the darkness.

He made another gesture for me to follow him, and he led me over the log, reaching back for my hand when I was nearly to the end. It was just gallantry; he dropped my hand again when I stepped off the log. Without speaking or accepting my offer of the flashlight, he led me swiftly out of the riverbed, and as we came to the meadow that lay just inside the trail-head, the moon came up. It wasn't quite full, but it looked huge above us. The fennel plants trembled and a bat twitched through the sky.

"Thank you," I said. "*Gracias.*"

He neither nodded nor shook his head. He leaned down and snapped off a tiny piece of an aloe plant, squeezed it, and then rubbed the blob of cold aloe on the scraped part of my shin. He stood up again and wiped the rest of the aloe on his pant leg. Though he'd just done something kind, I felt the distance between us the way, in science class, I sometimes felt the uncrossable space between planets.

He turned away and I heard, for a second or two, his light footsteps on the path. Whether he waited for me to unlock my bike and ride away, watching over me still, or whether he ran immediately back to his house in the woods I couldn't tell. He was too familiar with a life in hiding to let me know his position in the darkness.

I had a light on my bicycle, but that was just because my mother, my father, and I had once, when we were a normal, von Trappish family, taken our bicycles on camping trips and ridden along safe, carless paths to the ice cream stand. At no time in my life had I ever been permitted to ride my bike on Mission Road, where most things that couldn't go forty miles per hour—possums, squirrels, dogs, cats, coyotes, snakes, and rabbits—were promptly killed. It being Sunday night, there weren't many cars, but the ones that were on the road were screaming. Twice, cars flew by so close a rush of air pushed me slightly sideways, and I swore I would never, never do this again.

I decided I would hide the bicycle by Robby's tree house. If my mother was awake—and surely she would be—I would say I fell asleep in the tree house. Looking back, I see that I was beginning my practice with lies, preparing unconsciously for the day four months in the future when the fire would jump from tree to tree and roof to roof and I would head straight to the woods, to Amiel, to a house no fireman would think to defend but where all that I had come to love was in danger of burning alive.

Nineteen

I was too optimistic about my mother. She had checked the tree house. Repeatedly. She was waiting for me in a murderous mood.

"Where were you?"

"Greenie's."

"I called her."

"Yeah, I know," I said, in a vain attempt to bluff her.

"Where was Greenie, then, when she answered the phone?"

It didn't seem likely that I could guess this. "Okay. So I wasn't with her."

"The truth this time."

"I went for a bike ride."

"IN THE DARK?"

"I used the headlight."

"I don't understand what's gotten into you."

I expected her to say it was my father's fault. She thought

it, I suppose. What she said was that we were going to be spending a lot of time together. I was no longer grounded but *Siamesed*. For the remainder of my sentence, whenever I was not in school, I was going to be with her. All. The. Time.

"Fine," I said indifferently. It's harder for someone to punish you when you don't react. I went into Lavar's junky (but clean) bathroom, closed the door without slamming it, and started the bathwater. I stared at the plume of rust that went down the white enamel from the faucet to the drain, flipping at the still-cold water with my hand, and wondered what Amiel was doing now and if he had light of some kind in his house. I studied the stinging, shaved-off part of my shin. The aloe still glistened there, and I touched it carefully. I brought the trace of aloe to my nose to see if it had a smell, but it didn't, so I held my finger under the running water with the hope that I could wash away my longing.

Monday, Tuesday, Wednesday, and Thursday were sensationally long and boring, containing one conversation of note between Robby and me at school.

"I talked to Mary Beth last night," he said in his excessively casual way.

I tried to keep doing my geometry homework. "In person or on the phone?"

"Phone. I asked if she wanted to come over and swim."

Write out the formula for the perimeter of a triangle urged my book. "Is your dad gone or something?" I asked. *Isolate variable* x.

"No," Robby said. "He's not gone. But that's why I asked her over. It was a test."

"Oh," I said. "Super-clever."

"Thanks. She failed because she said she had to study for a biology test."

"Well, she does go to college," I told him. "She *could* study from time to time."

"Yeah, I thought of that. So I asked her what was going to be on the test." He lifted his chin in that weird way guys do when they're chin-waving at each other. "It turns out she's kind of smart."

He began to describe the biological concept of the chimera, which is the freaky real-world version of the mythological chimera: a monster made of different animals. While my lunch period floated away, he talked about gametes and zygotes and how a mule wasn't a true chimera and a hinny wasn't a true chimera (a hinny being a cross between a stallion and a jenny, whatever a "jenny" is), but a geep was.

"A geep?"

"Yes. Apparently, in 1984, a chimeric geep was made by combining embryos from a goat and a sheep."

"She told you that?"

"Well, no. I looked it up after we talked. But she talked intelligently about gametes and zygotes."

"How romantic."

"In another situation, maybe."

"So do you like her or what, Robby?"

"*Mais non, ma cousine.* I couldn't like someone who had affairs with married men. The main thing is to get her to like *me*."

"No offense, but why would a college girl like a guy in high school?"

"Why would a college girl like my dad?"

"Okay, so if she *does* like men who are either much too old or much too young, then what?"

"I'll tell her what I think of her."

At home, not even the appearance of three more silk eggs improved the mood between my mother and me as we went to the store together, sat in the cottage together, ate our canned soup together, and continued, without interest, our old sorority house ways—beds unmade, dishes unwashed, the fun of it gone because it was not a vacation but our lives.

On Thursday night, I wrote a note to Amiel, wrapped it in a plastic bag, then hid it in the underground box where I knew he would go in the morning to turn on the sprinklers in the grove.

Friday came, and I sat in the Oyster car with the windows open. Dew glazed the Icelandic poppies that held their platter faces to the gloom. Bits of morning fog fell very slowly, like petrified rain.

At the usual time, I heard the whirring of his wheels. Amiel parked his bike in the regular place, and I watched him in the rearview mirror until he retrieved the sprinkler key. Then Robby came out of his house and tossed his backpack into the car. "Are you feeling especially well grounded this morning?" he asked.

"I am," I said, unable to see Amiel or the sprinkler key or the plastic-wrapped letter. I breathed eucalyptus air and fog.

"Guess what I'm doing tonight?" he asked, exhaling mint and Listerine.

I saw a white-shirted flicker in the darkness of the trees. I didn't ask Robby what he was doing tonight, but he told me anyway.

"I have a *le* date," he said.

Robby was not a person who dated. He was a person who received phone calls from girls and never returned them, not even if they were honor roll, flute-playing girls from Advanced Orchestra class who wanted to practice the "Shepherd's Lament" for the state competition in Sacramento, and I would have thought he'd like those girls.

"Please tell me it's not MBF," I said. I was listening to what I imagined were Amiel's feet compressing layers of sodden leaves, never turning his face to the car where we sat, his body intent on grove work. I pictured him leaning down to open the water valves, seeing the letter in the plastic bag, picking it up.

Robby said mildly, "Okay. It's not MBF."

My mother came rushing out of the cottage with her commuter cup, purse, and keys, and off we went, past the avocado grove, through fog that obliterated people and things. I went to school without knowing whether Amiel had found my letter, but I felt pretty sure it was MBF that Robby was dating and that Robby had moved beyond the comic-book adventures of Tintin and his little dog Snowy into a weird father-son triangle of doom.

Twenty

I won't tell anyone anything.
I won't bother you.

The note said these things in Spanish:

No voy a decir nada a nadie.
No voy a molestarle.

I didn't sign my name but drew a little oyster holding a pearl—a code I'd been using with Greenie since fourth grade.

Midway through first period I became convinced that Esteban would find the letter before Amiel arrived and show it to my uncle. In second period, I imagined my uncle walking through the grove with Amiel to show him some problem or another, and they would get to the water valve and my uncle would see the bag with the note in it and pick it up. It would look much worse than it was: *nothing to nobody*. As if there was something big to tell.

All the time that I was thinking this and failing to write, correctly, the initials of the noble gases or compare and contrast, coherently, "The Emperor of Ice-Cream" with "Because I Could Not Stop for Death," Amiel was walking through the cathedrals of the grove, picking one hard green fruit after another, the heavy canvas bag rubbing his shoulder, the mass of it when filled with avocados as heavy and hard as a human body. He was also holding my letter in his back pocket and knowing exactly one more language than I thought he knew.

English.

Twenty-one

I've always been suspicious of those who say, *Things happen for a reason* and *What doesn't kill you makes you stronger*. Things happen all the time for no reason at all, and what doesn't kill you scares you witless.

I got a ride home with Hickey that Friday afternoon because my mother had to stay late for a meeting, and tired of being my Siamese twin all week, she said I could go with him. "But you'd better be there when I get home at five," she said. "With dinner prepared and the house tidied up," she added.

Hickey and Greenie were going to a movie in Temecula and I was glad, almost, that they had an excuse not to invite me.

"Just drop me here," I said at the bottom of my uncle's grove. Hickey didn't insist, and off they went, leaving me by myself at the fence. The chain link was too high to climb while wearing a backpack, so I went to the nearest locked gate and took a chance that I knew the combination. That's how I surprised them.

Two or three Hispanic guys, none I knew by name, were sitting on wooden crates and drinking from paper cups. Not far away was an RV that one of the workers lived in with his wife and two little boys, both of whom were sitting on the steps, watching Amiel. Amiel had drawn a circle in the dirt, and in the center of the circle he was juggling four balls, and the men were saying, "¡Más! ¡Más!" and longer words I didn't understand, though they seemed to be cheering him on. The little boys were smiling, and so was their mother, who stood just inside the open door of the RV.

Amiel bounced the balls on his chest in sequence and caught them one by one, then reached in his pocket. He held out two more balls and bowed, which made the little boys clap madly. The woman noticed me just then, and her gaze made the men turn their heads, and soon everyone, including Amiel, was staring at me.

"Hi," I said.

"Hola," one of the workers said, and I could feel them all wondering what I was doing here and what I would say to my uncle. It was three-thirty, and I had a general sense that the workday started at seven for everyone, since that's when it started for Amiel. There wasn't anything wrong with what they were doing after hours, but I didn't know how to say that.

One of the men started to pick up his crate and go, but the little boys were shrieking, "¡Más! ¡Más!"

Amiel made a gesture to the man, as if to say, "Sit down," and then he said to me, in a scratchy sort of English, "You can stay."

That he had spoken was surprising, more so that he spoke English, but that both of these things should be on my behalf filled me with a spreading liquid happiness. I sat down on my backpack and hugged my knees and was permitted to belong where I didn't belong. He juggled the six balls, and when they asked for *siete*, he juggled seven, then *ocho*, then the high-altitude popcorn explosion of nine. He bowed, and we clapped, and after he stowed the juggling balls in a canvas bag, they thought of more stuff for him to throw: avocados, oranges, and finally, long toy swords that the little boys brought from the house.

"Ay, *los cuchillos*," one of the men shouted, laughing.

Amiel nodded and slowly, with one eyebrow arched, put one sword between his teeth.

The little boys clapped and the men said, "*Andale*," which I couldn't translate, and Amiel juggled the toy blades for a while, throwing them high and catching them by the handles. He never missed, and we clapped, and then the woman started bringing out plates of rice and beef and salsa to us. One of the little boys brought Amiel and me cans of 7UP, but the men, I noticed, all drank beer.

The men talked to each other in Spanish while we ate, which was nice, though I caught nothing more than a few words, and when my watch said it was four-thirty, I stood up.

"Thank you," I said. "Thank you very much. I have to go home and make dinner."

They nodded, and as I walked away, I could hear them laughing and saying, "*¡Dale un machete! ¡No, DOS machetes!*" I knew what a machete was. I had grown up seeing workers cut branches with them like they were cutting butter, but I thought Amiel could juggle anything, so I didn't even look back.

Twenty-two

It was my mother who came to tell me one of the workers had cut his hand on a machete, who first saw Amiel holding his bloody hand on the driveway, and who remembered a doctor in town who did urgent care. While she was wrapping his hand with a towel that I brought, my aunt Agnès came out of her house and called my uncle, who didn't answer his phone. Despite the blood and glaring sunlight and confusion, I wondered where my uncle was and if he was with Mary Beth.

My aunt decided she would be the one to take Amiel to the doctor since she could speak Spanish as well as French and Italian, and when she opened the door of her immaculate Audi and told Amiel to sit on the leather seats that smelled of Agnès's musky vanilla Frenchwoman's perfume, she told me, "You come, too, Pearl. You can help me to find the address."

My mother couldn't very well say I was grounded, so I sat

down in the front seat and watched the workers who had sat on boxes during Amiel's juggling show, and who had evidently brought Amiel to the driveway, hang back with their arms folded. I wondered if they had goaded him into it or if he had wanted to impress them.

All the while the blood was soaking through the towel, and as my aunt was closing Amiel's door, she gestured for him to hold up his arm and said, "*Arriba del corazón.*" "Above the heart."

I remember, along with my fear and dread, my determination not to say that he'd been juggling and thereby prove my loyalty to Amiel. We reached at last the plain stucco building, the tinted glass door, the receptionist's pot of fake flower pens, the smell of cooked onions left over from someone's lunch, and the tall, skinny doctor taking Amiel right back. Agnès told me to go with Amiel while she arranged things in the front office. Her self-possession, her clothes, and her coldness were all working for us now. Whenever Agnès wanted to say that something was "impressive," she always said it was "impressing." That's what my aunt was, too. Very impressing.

When Amiel reached the white-papered bed in the white-shiny room, he started to faint. I was too far back to help, but the doctor must have thought that could happen because he caught Amiel in both arms. He asked me to help Amiel sit down, and when Amiel opened his eyes and stirred his legs, the doctor was unwinding the towel. Amiel's right index finger swelled on either side of a deep burgundy gash.

"How'd you do it?" the doctor asked him. He spoke

through a wispy brown mustache and studied Amiel through glasses that emphasized his baldness and fine, wrinkly skin. His voice was quiet and he wore a plaid shirt under his white coat.

I was going to say he was working in an avocado grove when Amiel said, in a low, raspy voice, "Machete."

"I'm going to have to see how deep it is," the doctor said. The gash was making me dizzy, and I would have liked to sit down on the floor.

"Why don't you hold on to his other hand," the doctor told me, so I took Amiel's left hand while Amiel looked away and, flinching, unwillingly tightened his grip. I looked away, too, once I saw the raw bone.

"It's not cut, the bone isn't," Dr. Woolcott said. "Still, you messed yourself up pretty good. Are you left-handed?"

Amiel looked confused.

"Do you understand English?"

Amiel nodded.

"I just wondered why you cut the right hand."

"He's got an injury to the throat," I said. "He doesn't talk much."

Dr. Woolcott accepted this and went to unwrap a hypodermic needle.

I've had stitches before, and I've had needles of thick numbing liquid eased into my gums like fiery arrows, but I've never had anything done to me like what I saw that day. Amiel held my hand because Dr. Woolcott told him to hold it while the fiery needles of pain were thrust into thin bony places, but then, during the black stitches, Amiel dropped my hand.

"What's wrong with your voice, son?" Dr. Woolcott asked as he washed his hands afterward.

"*Accidente*," Amiel whispered, using the Spanish form.

"What kind?"

"Esteering wheel," Amiel whispered, holding an invisible one with his good hand and showing how it had struck his neck.

"Laryngeal fracture," the doctor said, nodding to himself. "Where're you from?"

"México," Amiel said, the *x* that becomes *h* in Spanish softening further in his voice.

"Well, your hand should work okay when it heals," the doctor said. "Keep it clean. You'll need antibiotics and something for the pain."

My aunt, crisp and efficient in white linen, stood up when we approached the waiting room. She wrote a check from her beautiful wallet and smiled at the receptionist, the doctor, Amiel, and me.

"I pay for," Amiel told Agnès in the car. "How much?"

My aunt said it wasn't *necesario*.

Amiel insisted in English, and she refused in Spanish, and then they stopped talking.

We drove through downtown in silence, stopping only at the pharmacy to collect his prescriptions, and I tried to imagine Amiel gripping his handlebars with that swollen, stitch-filled finger as he rode his bicycle home. I was worried, too, about how he would keep a wound clean when he lived without a faucet. I knew I couldn't tell my aunt Agnès, or anyone else, that we needed to deliver Amiel to his camp on the river, but I couldn't stop myself from interfering, either.

"Aunt Agnès?" I said. "Doctor Woolcott said that Amiel shouldn't be alone for the first forty-eight hours. In case something goes wrong. Also, I don't think he can ride his bicycle."

My aunt Agnès trained her elegant eyes on Amiel's reflection in the mirror.

"*¿Vives solo?*" she asked.

Amiel lied. "No," he rasped. "*Estoy bien.*"

"*¿Dónde vives?*" she asked, so he told her part of the truth, and when we came to Willow Glen, she guided the smooth ginger car down through the narrow corkscrew of the canyon, gliding to the oak-dappled river, down, down, down, as the air-conditioning softly buffeted my face. She told Amiel, in her Spanish, something about her *esposo*, which even I knew to be "husband," and his *bicicleta*. Hoyt would bring the bicycle, I assumed, but where would he leave it? I didn't know.

We reached the bright emptiness of the dead end, where the aloe field lay in pale green stripes. Seven rusty mailboxes stood openmouthed in the heat. I couldn't help seeing them as Agnès did: she believed American mailboxes were disgraceful, worse even than our clothes. At the far eastern edge of the aloe field, you could see a little blue house, quaintly square like a playhouse or a shed, and beyond that, on a ridge, a trim yellow cottage.

My aunt was driving very slowly now, uncertain where to turn.

"*¿Dónde?*" she asked again, and Amiel clicked open his seat belt.

"*Aquí,*" he whispered.

Agnès stopped the car, and the engine ticked expensively at our feet. The sky was the color of birds' eggs and the river trees were green ink.

"*Gracias,*" I could barely hear him say, and I wondered if it hurt to speak or if he just found it difficult.

"*De nada,*" my aunt said, her expression confused. "I could take you all ways to your house," she said, bending her head slightly so that she could look through the windshield at the yellow house on the ridge.

Amiel shook his head, and when he closed the back door, he stood waiting for us to drive away, so Agnès made a careful circuit through the dirt circle where people parked when they came to hike the river. I kept watching him, and he watched us, long-limbed and silent, and the last thing I saw him do as my aunt pointed her car up the asphalt road was to remove from his back pocket a plastic bag, in which lay folded the white square of my letter. He didn't hold it up or smile or wave or wink. He didn't make any gesture at all besides holding the plastic envelope of my feelings so that I could see he had them, and then we drove away.

Twenty-three

"It is always the pity when my husband hires young ones," Agnès said to her windshield and me. "I tell him, *non*. The young ones, *non*. Only the married who are having other family here, like brothers and uncles. This one, he is new, *non?*"

She waited, so I said, "Yes."

She shook her head. "America. All friendly-friendly outside—'Hi! Bye! Have a nice day!' Beneath: nothing."

It was amazing to me that my uncle had persuaded this elegant, decisively critical person to leave Paris for Fallbrook. It had something to do with Western movies was all I knew. My uncle liked to joke that the real best man at his wedding should have been Clint Eastwood, who had apparently been the first dusty American to impress young, movie-watching Agnès Pleureux.

"Hmm," I said. I never liked to hear her thoughts on America.

Then she launched a zinger. "You are in love with him, *non?*"

I had never thought of Agnès as perceptive, maybe because to her I'd never been worth perception.

"No," I said flatly, inwardly ringing like a struck bell, and she shrugged.

"L'amour, la tousse, y la galle ne se peuvent celer!" she said with an amused smile. "The love, the cough, and the scab cannot be hidden!"

I coughed uncomfortably. It seemed to me that lots of scabs would be easy to hide if you kept your clothes on. I was going to argue that point, but she went on.

"It is not you, but the culture," she said with what I think was fondness, though it might have been amusement. "The culture says you cannot have, so you want. You think my *maman* was wanting American rancher for me?"

I was glad we'd switched to talking about her. "I'm guessing not."

"She tried to tell me that the tortoise cannot live with the parakeet."

I assumed she was the parakeet in this metaphor. "Is that another proverb?" I asked. Agnès was full of them. You'd think the French spoke in nothing but taglines for Aesop's fables. My favorite was the bizarre "You cannot teach old monkeys to make faces."

"*Non.* We had these animals in our house."

"Really? You had a tortoise?"

"*Oui!* Monsieur Pouf. He is still living with my *maman.* Do you know, tortoises they live for a hundred years or more? He wanders off, but we find him."

A strange image came to me of Agnès's mother, a beautiful freeze-dried flower of a woman in a gauze scarf, walking slowly through the Tuileries in search of a tortoise while my father passed by in one of his impeccable shirts, an impeccable lover on his arm. Would my father nod? Would he help look for Monsieur Pouf? I tried to think how many times my father might have encountered Agnès's family. Had there been three vacations there before I was born or just two?

I thought of confiding in Agnès so I could hear her thoughts about my father's departure and his attempt to lure me to Paris. I was afraid, though, that for Agnès the correct answer was always "yes" when offered an invitation to Paris.

We were idling at the place where Willow Glen met Mission Road. A bunch of animals grazed on the grassy slope beside us: pygmy goats, llamas, a miniature horse, a bristly pig, but no hinnies, mules, or misbegotten geeps. As often happened, cars were hurtling both ways on Mission Road, one after the other like missiles, and Agnès looked right, then left, then right, then left, watching for the gap that would allow us to dart out and join them. The car kept up its steady breathing of cool air on our legs, and I shivered. The angle of the sun illuminated the face of each driver in the cars heading west so that you saw, with weird clarity, each woman or man talking, thinking, worrying, squinting, or laughing and then folding down the visor to blot out the glaring sun. I watched each fleeting person as if they were characters in a silent movie, and then I saw someone I recognized: a pretty woman in a silver-green car, her chin tilted slightly up, her brown hair loose and wavy around her shoulders. Mary Beth Farlow didn't glance our way, just held the steering wheel with one hand, adjusted the visor, and raced past us toward the sun.

When we were safely on the road and headed in the direction from which Mary Beth's car had come, I felt the strangeness of knowing something I hadn't told.

"Young people do what they want always," Agnès said, turning briefly to glance at me. She wasn't smiling this time. Instead, she looked a little sad. "But I will tell you a saying my father told to me. *Amour fait beaucoup, mais argent fait tout.*"

I waited because the only word I understood was "love." "Which means?" I asked.

"Love does much," she said, "but money does all."

Twenty-four

On Saturday, my sentence was over. Still my mother didn't get up from her desk or leave, and as the hours passed, I felt like a helium balloon in her hand, bobbing around the house. Noon. One o'clock. Two. At two-thirty, she started to change her clothes for birding with Louise. "Are you and Greenie doing something tonight?" my mother asked.

"I don't know. I have to call her."

"I haven't seen her much. Did you have a fight?"

"No," I said. "She has a boyfriend."

"Is he nice?"

"Not really."

She applied lip balm, sunscreen, and a hat. "Want to come with us? The lagoon is beautiful this time of year."

"Nah," I said. "Sorry."

I could tell she was remembering the preschool me, the

one who cried and cried about being separated from her until finally she withdrew me from the program and let me stay home. Every day for the first week of blissful reunion, I clapped her cheeks, brought my lips close to hers, and said, "I can't get *enough* of you."

"Bye," I called out to her from the porch, and she hesitated, then walked away.

I stuffed my backpack with bottles of purified water, a tube of antibiotic cream, some Luden's Wild Cherry cough drops, and a roll of bandages so old they might have been Lavar's. They were still pretty clean, though.

I swung my leg over the bike and headed away from the house, anxious to see Amiel, but there in my path was my uncle, blasting toward me on his motorbike.

"Hey, Pearl," he said, stopping the bike and removing his helmet. "I understand you helped Abdiel yesterday."

"Amiel?" I asked.

"Yeah, Amiel. Agnès isn't too great with blood. Is he okay?"

I nodded.

"Hey, listen," he said. "I'm supposed to take his bicycle to him, right? That's what Agnès said."

"Uh-huh," I said. The backpack full of chilled water bottles pressed against my spine.

"You can show me where he lives, right? When did you become a cyclist, anyway?"

Part of Hoyt's charm was his constant question-asking. He was like a caffeinated gambler at a slot machine.

"I was just going for a ride," I said.

"Well, why don't you ride *his* bike, and I'll pick you up after you drop it off, okay?"

"Well, I guess I could."

"Tell me how far it is and so forth, the address, and I'll give you a head start. I'll come get you."

I shifted the weight of the bottles on my back and was alarmed by the loud bubbly sound they made.

"I was going to Greenie's afterward, though."

"Hey, that's no problem. I could take you there afterward."

"Well, it's not . . ." I wasn't good at improvisation. I paused as if I were working out a logistical problem. "You know, I think I could walk from where Amiel lives to Greenie's, really. And then her mom could take me home."

"You sure?"

"Yeah! Positive. I'll just, you know, get a ride back."

"You call me if she can't give you a ride, okay? I'll come get you. Maybe buy you a donut."

While my uncle watched, I climbed onto Amiel's bicycle. I waved goodbye. I rode over the freeway and up Mission with cars swishing past me every two seconds, and then I peeled away to coast down into river world, where I was about to break my promise to Amiel about not bothering him.

The oak trees along the road were black-limbed and the air was cold. Now and then a squirrel streaked across my path or a crow pecked at a walnut on the blacktop, flapping away just before my tires reached the bits of broken shell. It was so quiet I could hear their feathers like a woman's taffeta dress.

I knew the trail by now, and riding was much faster than walking, so when I found myself at his bend of the river, I was panting. I walked the bike through the current and then pushed it over sand that breaded the tires like white cornmeal.

Now what? I wondered. *Call out to him?*

There's something about trespassing that makes you feel larger than everything else, and clumsier. I pushed Amiel's bicycle to the lattice of gray branches and considered just leaning it there for him to find, but I couldn't leave his only expensive possession in plain sight.

"Amiel?" I half whispered. "I've brought your bike."

I touched the wall with my fingers and listened to my loud heartbeat. He didn't answer, and I stood very still. I stared at the branches under my fingertips, where tiny white cobwebs pillowed all the crevices and an orange speckled orb weaver ascended a line he'd just made.

"Amiel?" I called softly, and then I made myself look around the corner.

He sat with his knees up on the blankets that formed his bed. The fatness of the white bandages on his hand glowed in the shadowy room, but I couldn't see if his eyes were open or closed. "I'm sorry," I said. "I was worried. I know I said I wouldn't bother you."

At that he turned his head, but he didn't answer.

I stepped forward and opened my backpack. I set the water, the tube of antibiotics, and the roll of bandages on the ground. "I brought your bike back. That way my uncle didn't have to know. Where you live, I mean."

All that was left to show him was the Luden's cough drops. My mouth was so dry that I unwrapped one and popped it in. I held one out to him and he took it, but you can't unwrap a cough drop with one hand. I sat down and took it back, and after I had untwisted the wrapper, I gave it to him.

"Do you want me to go?" I asked.

He didn't shake his head, and he didn't nod. He put the cough drop in his mouth.

I waited, and as I waited, I kept my eyes averted, as if I would only be invading his privacy if I *looked* at his things. I studied the trees and wondered if the bird that was singing was a finch or a phoebe, the dark sugar dissolving on my tongue. Finally, I felt so awful about the silence that I looked him full in the face and saw that he'd closed his eyes. That seemed peculiar. He was resting the bandaged hand on his knees, which were pulled up, and it seemed like a position you might sit in if you felt sick or hopeless. "Does it hurt?" I asked.

He shook his head, but he didn't open his eyes.

Maybe it was because I was sitting there in his camp, instead of seeing him at my uncle's ranch, that I realized, for the first time, the loneliness of his life. To me, the river was a romantic place where you could live like Thoreau or Laura Ingalls Wilder. But when I tried to imagine going off on my own to a foreign country and making a house out of scraps and looking for work and eating ramen noodles for every meal, the canyon seemed dirty and hard and cold. I reached out my hand to touch one of his fingers, but I was just grazing the skin when he opened his eyes and pulled it back.

He studied me with his face tensed. *"Imposible,"* he said, a more beautiful word in Spanish but just as final.

"Right," I said. "You don't feel that way about me."

He closed his eyes again, then opened them. "Go away," he said pleadingly. *"Por favor."*

"Okay," I said.

I stood up and blundered out into the sunlight, which reminded me of the problem his bike presented. I pointed to the bicycle, and he nodded. Holding his cut hand unnaturally still and stiff, he wheeled the bicycle to a place in the willows where it could hardly be seen. Then he turned to me, and I stood awkwardly for a few seconds, waiting to feel less horrible. He just stared at me with his solemn, narrow, beautiful face all sunken with pain and something else.

"Goodbye," I said.

I held out my left hand as if to shake his left hand, and at first he didn't move. Then he took my hand and held it as if we were going to shake like normal strangers, moving our arms up and down politely, but instead we were still. We stood like that, hand in hand, and it reminded me of what happens when you join circuits on a circuit board. The current travels and the bulb of light begins to glow.

Then he disconnected us, and the light went out.

Twenty-five

This was the day that I discovered a very useful thing: the river is a huge crack in the landscape of Fallbrook. There is the civilized world of groves and corrals and houses and yards, all of them on hilltops because people like views, but far below those hilltops and streets, in a dark, winding cut, lay the river world. You could hike straight into that world through marked gates, like the one on Willow Glen, or you could just climb down into it from the yards on the hilltops. And I learned this by climbing *out* of river world into the backyard of the house where Greenie lived with her brother and her parents and a dog named Poochie that fortunately remembered me.

Greenie and Hickey were sitting on her back deck when I came trespassing out of the peach trees. It was almost fully dark by then, and the evening mist coated leaves and grass.

I had scratched both forearms, my shoes were full of dirt, and my hair felt like a dried plant sculpture.

"What the *le feck?*" Greenie said. She'd learned a little Franglish from Robby and me.

"Hello *le bonjour*," I said. Poochie was a lapdog trapped in a Doberman's body, so after barking briefly, she tucked her nose into my hand and lifted it impatiently, as if to say, "The hand is for petting me."

Hickey stood up, too, and came lazily to the rail of the deck. He was wearing a ski cap that pressed his bangs into his eyelashes, and he casually hooked one finger in Greenie's nearest belt loop. "Are you a werewolf or an amateur cat burglar?" he asked. He sounded hopeful about both, so I didn't answer.

"If you want to come over and visit me, we still have a front door," Greenie said.

I said that I was hiking and got tired, so I found a shortcut.

"Hiking?" Greenie said. "Again? What's with you and the river these days?"

"Can I have one of those?" I asked. She and Hickey were sipping from brown bottles that I was relieved to see contained root beer, not real beer, probably because Greenie's parents were home. Once I'd climbed the steps onto the deck, I could see the backs of their heads silhouetted by the television screen and hear sweeping orchestral music.

Greenie went inside and got me a root beer. I stayed where I was so that Mr. and Mrs. Coombs wouldn't pose their usual questions about how my mother was getting along.

"So how're you lovebirds?" I asked with false cheer. Since only old people use the word *lovebirds*, I immediately went quiet. Hickey and Greenie re-entwined themselves on the wooden swing, and I perched on the edge of a ratty lounge chair. I wondered if the Barbie wedding lodge was still in Greenie's basement. We'd glued the Lincoln Logs together on a piece of particleboard so the building wouldn't fall down if there were an earthquake during the reception. The Barbie health and safety code was pretty rigorous.

"Hickey wants to go to some club in Oceanside," Greenie said, "but I told him my curfew's too early." She tossed her head in the direction of her parents, and I wondered if what made her look so different tonight was the back-from-the-dead eye shadow or her new Hickey-length bangs. "I think we should just go to that Paddy O'Whatsit's pub downtown and eat fried chips or whatever they call them. Wanna be our chaperon?"

I didn't. I wanted to go down to the basement and be nine years old. I wanted to make some miniature wedding cakes out of Sculpey clay, eat popcorn with real melted butter, drink Swiss Miss hot chocolate in Greenie's kitchen, and then fall asleep in a plaid sleeping bag that smelled like cedar chips.

"Nah," I said. "I don't want to ruin your date."

"You wouldn't," Greenie said. I sort of believed her, and I think she sort of meant it.

Hickey just took a long drink of soda. In the yellow light of the porch his freckles disappeared. He was a pale, angular sign that everything in my life had changed. "Maybe we could find a *le* dude for you," he said. "One who's into stealth-hiking."

"Come *on*," Greenie said. "Celebrate the end of your house arrest."

Mostly I went because I didn't want to call my uncle, and Hickey said he'd take me home at ten if I didn't go AWOL on them again. Greenie tried to get me to put a pound of eye shadow on my eyelids, but I just brushed the twigs out of my ugly hair and stopped looking in the mirror at the face that of course Amiel didn't love, and we rode in semi-silence to the quiet center of our quiet town, where the new streetlights were those ochre-yellow kind that suck the color out of things. As we were walking by a gnarled pepper tree that grows right in the center of the mostly empty parking lot, I saw a familiar car. It wasn't red in this light—the light bled the color out of it—but it was definitely the Honda Fabricationist.

"That's Robby's birthday present," I said to Greenie.

"No kidding?" she said. "I thought you said his birthday was kind of a downer."

"It was," I said. "It definitely was."

Paddy O'Hara's used to be the Packinghouse, a steak-and-salad place where the booths were covered in red vinyl. When you were sitting in the booth drinking a root beer with lemon in it (and sometimes also a maraschino cherry), you could read all the framed orange crate labels from when Fallbrook was the home of Lofty Lemons and Red Ball Oranges. When you went to the bathroom, it was like you were going to a museum, there were so many enlarged gray photographs of the real packing-house and the people who worked there in the 1930s and '40s, and you could get really close to their faces and wonder if they were truly happy or just looked that way for the camera. The ceilings were low and cozy then, made of that fancy tin that looks like metal doilies, and the tables were packed close together except for the big round booths in the corners where I liked to sit. The main waitress was this woman named Maureen that my father knew from Fallbrook High School, where they'd apparently had typing class together, and she would say that I was looking more like my father all the time, even though most people don't say that. I always picked the Packinghouse for my birthday dinner, and Maureen always put extra whipped cream on my hot fudge brownie sundae and my mother told me to wish for something that couldn't be bought or sold.

The ceilings of the new restaurant were at least twenty feet high and the crate labels were gone and one side of the restaurant was filled with a giant mahogany Irish-style bar. The biggest television I'd ever seen was broadcasting a basketball game, and when Greenie turned her head and saw who was playing, she groaned. "Let's go somewhere else," she said, pulling on Hickey's arm. "It's the Rockets," she told me. "Hickey's true love."

But Hickey was leading her to a table, so we followed him. I didn't see Robby anywhere, but I remembered there used to be a long, narrow dining room on the other side of the Packinghouse, through the doorway beside the bar that was still labeled RESTROOMS. Greenie stared gloomily at the menu and Hickey watched the Rockets. "I think I'll have the stew," I said finally. "I'm going to the bathroom."

An odd thing happened on my way. There was still a

dining nook tucked on the other side of the wall, but those tables were empty. No TV, no Rockets, no eaters, no Robby or his date. What I remember next was a passageway that looked exactly the same as it had when I was little. Same old pictures of smiling lemon packers, same old conveyor belts of tumbling fruit, same old Lofty Lemons crate label in a cheap wooden frame. The door to the kitchen was open, like those doors usually are, and I felt hungry and sick at the same time, as if my head were filling up with noble gases. My left temple started to ache, and I pressed my hand over that eye to make it stop. I thought I might faint, the way I did one time in fourth grade after I ran all the way to Mrs. Gilliland's class from the kickball field. I leaned against the wall with my hand over one eye and remembered what I told Hickey about my prophetic eyeballs.

"Blue sees you here, brown sees where you're going to wind up."

It was fry-grease hot in the hallway, and the kitchen workers, all Hispanic, sweated as they carried and chopped. The eye I'd covered was the blue one, and I tried to see, with my brown eye, something other than moving bodies in white aprons, stained tin pots, brown rubber doily mats, and giant tubs of grease. The passageway felt darker and longer, tilted crazily on its side, and then I couldn't see the kitchen anymore. My mind filled with the sound of rushing water and the next thing I felt was the wall. I had steered myself smack into it, I guess. Fortunately, no one saw me. I just stood up and felt my way to the door that said LASSES. It took me a while to feel normal again—I splashed my face at the dingy sink, ate a Luden's I found in my pocket, tried looking one-eyed into the mirror for

137

someone other than myself—but I finally had nowhere to go but back to Greenie and Hickey and the big television set.

Greenie jumped out of her chair when I came back. "There you are!" she said semi-hysterically. "We were just about to move to another table. On the non-television side!"

Hickey was standing but not enthused. Greenie put her hands on my shoulders to steer me, as if I might resist, but I stepped on something I thought was a foot and turned to apologize. That's when I saw what Greenie was trying to protect me from seeing.

My father was standing at the bar. He'd just finished saying something to the bartender, who nodded, and then my father turned and saw me standing like the last pin on a bowling lane.

It's funny how his smile seemed completely sincere. "There you are!" he said, just like Greenie had. For a second, his face was the old face. Maureen the waitress was gone and the booths were gone, but it was the old him and the old me, the one that loved him more than all the world.

"Your mom called Greenie's," he said, working his way over to us, "and they said you were here."

I didn't answer. He kissed my cheek. I kissed his cheek, too.

Already Greenie and Hickey were fading away from us, melting back from a parent they didn't have to listen to.

"My car's out back," my father said. "You guys need a ride somewhere?"

"No, we're good," Hickey said.

I hadn't ordered anything, but I didn't like how my dad just assumed I was leaving with him now.

"What about the food?" I asked Greenie.

"The waitress hasn't taken our order yet," she said. "It's taking a zillion years."

"You're hungry?" my dad asked, which I have to say was a silly question. Why else does a person go to a restaurant? "We can eat here, if you want. Remember the Packinghouse? I can't believe how much nicer it is in here now. What a change."

"Never mind," I said. "I'm not that hungry."

We walked out into the parking lot together, and I eyed Robby's Honda under the murky pepper tree—still there, still dark—but I didn't point it out. My father led me well beyond the cars clustered near the back door of Paddy O'Hara's and the neighboring Café Chartreuse to a solitary Mercedes parked diagonally across two spaces about ten leagues from everyone else. I'd never seen the car before.

"A rental?" I asked.

"Lease to own," he said.

I absorbed this information as he pushed a button on his key and the car lit itself up inside.

"Like it?" he said.

I didn't speak.

He opened the door for me and I got in. The car already smelled like the black licorice I knew would be in the glove compartment if I opened it. He started showing off the features—GPS, surround sound—but I said, "I get it. It's a nice car. A lot nicer than our health insurance."

"Ah," he said, easing himself back in the driver's seat. "That's what you're mad about?"

I didn't say anything because it was hard to talk to my father as if he were an idiot. He couldn't be both my father and an idiot. I wouldn't allow it.

"The resentment you seem to feel is not fair," my father said in his controlled angry voice, the voice that when I was very little made me curl up behind the clothes in my closet instead of in my bed, where I felt I didn't deserve to sleep. "This car is a tool. A tool that shows clients I know what good investments are. This car says, 'Trust me.' "

I never could fall asleep in the closet, but I stayed there for hours, until long after the television laugh tracks and the rattling sound of my mother's vitamins tumbling into her hand.

"As for health insurance, when your mother and I were together," he went on, "I did more than my fair share of everything. For fifteen years, I worked ten hours a day. I did work I hated because that was my role: to earn the money that paid for everything everyone wanted. It was her job to—well, I wouldn't really call it a job. It was more like a lot of hobbies that she treated as if they were jobs, even though none of them earned a dime. And that meant there was never time for me to do anything that made *me* feel happy. I realized, finally, that I couldn't go on living like that. I don't think anyone should. If your mother now has to comprehend what it takes to stay solvent month to month, how to pay for the boring things like doctor bills and car insurance as well as heirloom hollyhocks and hand-spun yarn from the women's cooperatives of Boola

Boola, East Africa, well—better late than never. We all have to grow up sometime. Life isn't just doing whatever you want to do because you find it meaningful and sincere, while someone else does the mind-blowingly repetitive, corporate sellout *work* that pays for things like health insurance and also, yes, this car."

I had nothing to say to this. I looked hard at the sulfur streetlight on the other side of the parking lot, which was the same noxious color he shone on our life. I knew that my father did practical things and my mother did creative things, but I thought that was okay with both of them.

"Do you want to get something to eat?" my father asked. He spoke softly, as if all that anger could be forgotten now.

"No," I said.

"So you just want me to take you home." There was an edge to his voice again, and I knew he thought I was being a pill. I *was* a pill. I was a pill so big he couldn't swallow it.

"I guess," I said. I wondered where he was staying the night. He started the car, and in the moment that he began to drive slowly across the parking lot, the door to the Café Chartreuse opened and two people stepped out. One was a woman, and the other was Robby. I hoped that if I kept my mouth shut, my father wouldn't recognize Robby, but the streetlight shone fully on their faces as we approached.

"Hey. Who's that with Robby?" my father asked.

"I don't know," I said. Mary Beth had glanced into our car, and so had Robby. We were trapped.

My father stopped the car and rolled down both of our

141

windows. "I thought that was you, Robby," he said. "Sorry I missed your birthday party."

"No problemo," Robby said. Mary Beth was standing at a slight distance from Robby with her hands in the pockets of her coat. She looked as if she were hoping to remain anonymous, but my father stuck his hand out the window in her direction and said, "Pleased to meet you. I'm Robby's uncle, Glen DeWitt."

"Mary Beth," she said, smiling as she had when she was handing out slices of Robby's cake. It was a reserved, strictly courteous smile. She offered it to me and nodded slightly.

"Enjoying the Fallbrook nightlife, huh?" my father asked.

"I just got off work," Mary Beth said.

"How's Paul doing?" my father asked, indicating the café and Mr. Eckert with a little nod. I wondered if my father had ever complained, when he was at the café without me, about what a drag it was to have a wife and a child, something Mr. Eckert might have remembered when I told him my father had moved out.

"Oh, he's fine," Robby said. "He asked about you."

This led nowhere, maybe because my father knew people in town weren't likely to take his side. There was an awkward pause, and then my father said, "So where are you headed now?"

I thought this was a little nosy, but Robby looked unperturbed, maybe even glad to lay out his plans. "I promised to show Mary Beth three things in Fallbrook she didn't know existed but that she will *definitely* like."

"Three?" I asked.

"That sounds ambitious," my father said.

"I lack no confidence," Robby said, and this appeared to be true. When he raised a hand to wave at us, Mary Beth waved and followed him to the car under the pepper tree, leaving me alone again with my father.

"So where are you staying tonight?" I asked, and then regretted it, not really wanting to imagine his preferred life.

"Our new condo," he said.

"Our what?"

"A condo in San Diego. We sold a little triplex in Scottsdale and needed the other leg of a ten thirty-one exchange, so I thought, hey, why not buy myself something that would be a good investment *and* keep me within striking distance of my little girl? I was hoping you'd come and stay with me for the weekend, see what kind of furniture you'd like to put in the second bedroom."

I wasn't sure what he meant by "we." Usually, that meant him and his business partner. But now it might mean him and the person who owned the apartment in Paris. It certainly didn't mean my mother.

"Oh. There's something I have to do tomorrow," I said.

"Can't it wait? I was really looking forward to spending the weekend with you."

"It's a big project," I said. "It's half my grade."

"Why don't I just drive by the house, you pick up your books and whatever you need, and you can work on the project in the condo? There's this big window overlooking the bay. You can see Coronado Island. The aircraft carriers. Little white sailboats. It's beautiful, I'm telling you. I have a desk right by the window where you can sit."

"I would," I said, "but it's a group project."

"Okay," he said, giving up. "Next time."

"Yeah," I said. "Next time."

Twenty-six

My mother was sitting at the desk when I came in that night, a bowl of cocoons beside her computer.

"How were the birds?" I asked.

"We saw a grebe," she said. Then she went back to considering the cocoons. There were nine little white ovals even though she'd started with twenty-five worms, and based, my mother said, on the research she'd been doing all evening, she would need to kill them if she wanted to get the silk off the cocoons in one unbroken strand.

"What do you mean, 'kill them'?"

My mother looked glumly at a page of text on her screen. "I guess they bake them at silk factories. They bake most of them, anyway. A few of them they allow to go through metamorphosis or there wouldn't be any eggs at the end of the cycle."

We were both silent for a few seconds. Then I said, "So the worm builds the cocoon in order to become a butterfly—"

"A moth, actually," my mother said. She showed me a picture of a white moth. It had a black dot on each wing and a face that seemed mostly mustache. It was nothing you'd want to prevent from entering the world.

"It eats twenty-four hours a day for three weeks to build the cocoon to become a beautiful furry *moth*," I said, "but then you kill it while it's still a worm."

"Uh-huh," she said. "But Louise says she tried it one time and the stench was terrible. You're supposed to bake them at a low temperature for a long time—all day, I think, or maybe a few days, and she said she almost had to burn down the house, the smell was so awful."

"Ugh," I said. "Don't you think that's a sign that you shouldn't kill stuff for thread?" I gently touched one of the cocoons. "How much silk would you really be getting out of this, anyway?" I asked.

"Well, each strand is a mile long."

We looked at the cocoons. Each one was smaller than my thumb.

"Don't worry. I'm not going to bake the dear cats," my mother said. Early on in her research, she'd discovered that people who are fanatical about raising silkworms call them "cats," which is short for *caterpillars*. "But you know, the moth doesn't have that much to look forward to. The silk business is easier if the moths can't fly, so the bad fliers have been preserved over the centuries while the good fliers have been killed. Apparently, when the moth eats its way out of the cocoon, it will just wait for a mate right there in the same spot. You don't need a net or a cage or anything. The moth will mate, or not mate, and if it's a female, it will lay eggs, and then it will die. It will never even fly across the room."

"Maybe silk isn't the business for us," I said, fingering the cocoon I liked best. It was actually two cocoons bound up together because the second silkworm to spin itself into a cottony tomb had lashed herself to an existing egg—that of her lover, I liked to think—as if to make sure she could find him when they woke up in totally different bodies.

I tried to slip away to brush my teeth, but she closed the computer, stood up, turned to me, and asked me warily, "Aren't you going to tell me how it went with your father?" My mother had her hair pinned up and she was wearing a pair of dingy slippers with flannel pajama pants. Over the pants she wore a big chenille hooded sweater that made her look smaller and somehow younger. She'd been getting smaller over the past few months, anyway. She didn't cook, so we didn't eat much, and she'd started running again, something she'd never had time for when my father was around.

"What size are you now?" I asked.

"Don't avoid the question."

"He invited me to stay the weekend at his new condo in San Diego."

"His what?"

I told her what I could remember about taxes and the ten thirty-one exchange.

"I don't *believe* it. I just don't believe it. Of all the—" She stopped. She was a color I hadn't seen before, a scary shade of wax. "Go outside, will you please?" she asked. "No. I'll go outside. You stay here. Don't follow me."

I stayed where I was for a few seconds after she shut the door, and then I went to the lamp. I turned it off. I flipped the switch in the kitchen, too. In the darkness of the messy living room, I made my way to the window to make sure she was all right. In the moonlight you can see all sorts of things, and I saw my mother walking furiously under the avocado trees, kicking at the leaves so they flew up around her. I saw her hit one of the trees with the side of her fist and grab a branch and shake it really hard, as if she'd like to rip it from the trunk, but it was too big, so it barely moved. Lavar's house wasn't soundproof, so I heard every name she called him, and I heard her say the most painful thing of all, "Oh, I wish I'd never, ever been born."

I should have gone outside and hugged her, as she would have hugged me, but for some reason I couldn't. The child-me that had patted her cheeks and kissed her, where had she gone? I stayed still like the tree trunks until she wiped her cheeks and crossed her arms and started back up the front steps. Then I did the only thing I could do that I thought might make her feel better. I stretched out on the foldout couch that I hadn't bothered for several days to fold up and I pulled the wrinkled sheets and blanket over every part of me, even my head, so that when she came in the house, she could pretend I was fast asleep and knew nothing at all about how he hurt her.

Twenty-seven

I dreamed I spun myself into a white chamber with no doors or windows using my own hair, which turned white as I pulled a single strand of it from my temple and moored myself to the white egg beside me that I thought contained Amiel, but when I broke free of the shell I'd waited in for what seemed like years, the white egg had a hole in it like the end of a kaleidoscope, and when I looked through it, I saw that he was dead.

The noise that I heard through the real cocoon of my blankets was my uncle pounding on the door, shouting at me to get dressed because we were getting donuts while they were still hot.

I struggled to the door and gave the first excuse I could think of, and the least probable. "I'm on a diet," I said.

He laughed out loud. "We'll get you the diet donut!" he

said. "Where's your mother? Tell her I'll buy her a donut, too. You can either be thin or happy, right?"

I wondered how this applied to Frenchwomen. I shuffled to my mother's room and considered the evidence, which mostly amounted to strewn clothes and sheets. I trudged back to the porch. "She must've gone running," I said. I wished at that moment that I was running, too, pounding along dirt that other people had pounded into a trail.

I washed my face. I brushed my teeth. I glumly followed my uncle to the Packrat, where Robby was sitting with his eyes closed. He dutifully extracted himself from the cab so I could take my seat in the middle. "*Bonjour le* you," he said. "*Bonjour le* donuts."

Sunday mornings always felt so much cleaner, as if the windows of the world had been washed. Mission Road was empty, and just ahead of us a coyote appeared, its coat all rumpled and thick like a German shepherd's, its eyes, as it turned to regard us, both haunted and indifferent.

"So, Robby," my uncle Hoyt began. "Your mother said you went on some sort of date last night, huh?"

"Yep," Robby said. He nodded. I studied the olive trees on one side of the road. Nobody ever harvested olives, not even my uncle, and yet they grew everywhere in Fallbrook. I made a mental note not to point out this untapped market to my mother.

"Nice girl?" my uncle prodded.

"Yep," Robby said.

"Someone from school, I guess?"

"Older," Robby said.

"What's her name?"

"Mary."

"Mary. Okay. What'd you do?"

We reached the crest of a hill and I could see the place on the horizon called the Sleeping Indian, a huge land formation that looked, once you'd heard the name, exactly like an earthen man stretched out on his back. Beyond his body, on clear mornings like this one, you could see the line of blue that was the ocean.

"I gave her a tour of unknown Fallbrook," Robby said. He was looking out the window as we passed Willow Glen, and part of me leaped out of the car and started walking north.

"Sounds good," Hoyt said. "What does that mean, exactly?"

"First we took a little walk," Robby said, nibbling a little at the edge of his thumb.

"You took a walk at night?"

"Downtown. I took her along the promenade."

I knew this was something Hoyt would be glad to hear about. He was a big one for civic projects, and his name was on the plaque honoring the men and women who'd donated time and money to the promenade, a half-finished path that led from the library to Fallbrook Street. For three blocks, you could stroll along a path of wood chips, maples, sycamores, and oaks. The landscape committee had planted hibiscus, too, and passionflowers and fortnight lilies and bougainvillea. They had installed trash cans and informative signs and benches that vandals beat with what appeared to be iron crowbars in the middle of the night. On one side of the newly planted trees, the land dropped away into a creek bobbing with trash left by teenagers who wrote unpronounceable gang signs in black spray paint on the concrete, but you could also see white egrets and the occasional duck. On the far side of the creek, little stucco houses that looked like they'd been in Fallbrook back when it was just a bunch of lemon farms stood in the shade of far older trees, and in the tiny yards, prickly pear cactus plants made fences for goats, chickens, and, in one yard, a pig. Unfortunately, most of the people who used the promenade in the daytime were scary men in possession of liquor bottles, so I hadn't walked there in a while.

"She'd never seen the promenade?" Hoyt asked.

"Nope," Robby said.

"I thought you said there were three things," I said to Robby.

"Right," Robby said. We were approaching town now. The truck idled between El Toro Market and Gilberto's taco shop and M & M liquor store with its signs for phone cards to Mexico and Western Union and Corona beer and strange Mexican candies flavored with chili and tamarind. Sunlight made everything look new and hopeful. "Number two was the bridge to poverty," Robby said.

"The what?" my uncle asked, turning left with the green arrow that sent us slowly along Main Street, past the Got Holes tattoo parlor and piercing gallery, the Mexican clothing stores that displayed dresses on transparent torsos hung outside the doors, the *panadería* that sold *menudo* on Wednesdays and every day sold sugar-sanded cookies as thick as cinnamon rolls. After the *panadería*, the Mexican businesses just stopped and the places we normally shopped began: Village Sports, Village Vac, Village Shoes.

Robby said, "That iron bridge that goes from the promenade over the creek."

"Well, that's kind of a dark name for it," Hoyt said.

I had to agree that the bridge was a little strange. I remember thinking, when Hoyt took us to see it, that someone had gone to a crazy amount of trouble to make a footbridge maybe five people would ever use. The sides of the iron bridge were a cutwork pattern of reeds and herons and egrets. It didn't lead anywhere except from the promenade to the stucco houses fenced with prickly pears, and you couldn't see it from Main Street.

"What else?" my uncle asked. He was a little puzzled, I could tell.

"I thought she'd like number three best of all," Robby said, "but it was the wrong time of day."

We waited. My uncle pulled into the parking lot and I could smell the scalded sugar smell of the donut shop. Sunlight bounced off all the cars as Robby said, "Took her to see the ostrich. Unfortunately, the ostrich was asleep."

Twenty-eight

My mother had a job interview that afternoon, so she was trying on clothes when I came home. My clothes, actually. All of her pants were too loose, she said, so she was rummaging through my closet, which used to be Lavar's coat closet and was too packed and disorganized for easy rummaging. "Where's the job?" I asked.

"Oh, it's a bookstore," she said.

"Which bookstore?"

"One of the chains," she said.

"That sounds fun," I said. "You like books."

"Yeah!" she said. I could tell she didn't think it would be fun.

"Does that pay more than subbing?" I asked.

"It will be in *addition* to subbing," she said. "The opening is for evenings and weekends. That's why my interview is on a Sunday. Besides, it's almost summer, remember?"

"You're going to work two jobs?"

"Until summer," she said. "Why are these clothes so wrinkled?" she asked.

"Because we never iron them," I said.

She found a brown skirt and a pleated white blouse that I hadn't worn for a long time because Greenie said it made me look like a librarian, and my mother told me to turn on the iron.

"Maybe I should get a job," I said, watching her apply the eyeliner, wipe it off, and draw another shaky line. Both of her eyes were blue, which made her homochromic. This was a word we used to toss around as a family when we were a family.

"If you were sixteen and had a license," my mother said, going at the lips now, "it would be easier. Or if we lived in town so you could get to work without a car."

My birthday was in November.

She stepped into a pair of black heels I'd chosen for homecoming back in the fall and hadn't worn since. My father had pinned on my corsage and kissed both my ears, a routine he'd started when I was little, and then I got into the backseat of Eldon Barton's mother's car and pretended not to notice that Eldon's hands were shaking. I still saw him at school sometimes and we ignored one another.

My mother jabbed an earring into each of her earlobes.

She lifted her hair to study the effect. "Oh my God," she said. "My ears have gotten old."

I said this was ridiculous, and I leaned close to see that she *did* have wrinkles on her earlobes. "Nah," I said. "Ears don't age."

She let her hair fall back over the wrinkles and sighed. "I'm off," she said.

"You look pretty," I said. Losing weight did make her look pretty. It just didn't make her look happy. Maybe my uncle was right about that.

When she was gone, I had three choices: homework, moisturizing my earlobes, or a moth-to-the-flame ride down to the river. Amiel's insistence that I go away, *por favor*, still stung, so I sat on the sofa and studied the room. What a mess the house was. I lay back on the bed and closed my eyes. The project I'd told my father about was half truth, half lie. We had nine days of school left, and four of them would be devoted to tests.

For a while, I did geometry, and then I began reading— cross-legged and pillow-supported—a chapter about the War of 1812 that beckoned me, ever so softly, into the early stages of sleep, blurring the sunlight on the sofa and the glossy page and the backs of my hands, and I remember that when my phone rang its way into my sleep, there was too much glare on the tiny screen of the phone for me to see Greenie's name displayed there in tiny insistent letters.

"Calling to report weird phenomenon," she said.

"What's that?"

"Well, Hickey's mom belongs to the Land Conservancy, you know?"

"No."

"And they were having this big Clean Up the River campaign today, and she made Hickey go with her because she says all he ever does is hang out with me until late at night and then sleep for, like, eternity the next day, and she thinks he's going to get juvenile diabetes from lack of exercise."

I thought his mom probably had more to worry about than juvenile diabetes, Hickey being the bony type, plus I was pretty sure he was fabricating the love with Greenie, but I didn't say anything. I pictured the river instead. I saw a bunch of people armed with orange plastic bags and trash pokers gathering around Amiel like a haz-mat team.

"I told him his mother should take *you* next time," Greenie said, "since you could be, like, Miss River Hike of the Santa Margaritaville, and he said he would definitely pass on your name as a potential member."

"Thank you," I said.

"Anyway, Hickey's going along picking up garbage, and he's texting me every few seconds to tell me the disgusting nature of trash he's found, and like five seconds ago I get a message that says he's found some letter you dropped on the trail."

I had just picked up the joined pair of silkworm cocoons and was trying to see inside them. "A letter *I* dropped on the trail?" I asked. I set the cocoons down. "What are you talking about?"

"I don't know. A letter. With your name on it. He didn't, like, open it."

"Why not?"

"It wasn't addressed to him, dummy. He's a respectful person. It was addressed to you, I guess."

"To me? It said *Pearl DeWitt* and my address and everything? Was there a stamp on it?"

"I don't know. He just said there was this really thick envelope with the name Pearl on it. He knows you go there, like, hourly, and it's not like Pearl is a common name if you're under the age of eighty-nine. So he figured you were the Pearl in question."

I couldn't think what it was. There were the notes I'd written to Amiel, of course, but I hadn't used envelopes. Would Amiel use an envelope?

"So where is Hickey now?" I asked.

"Out on the trail, poking more trash. He's picking me up after, so we'll come over."

"When will that be?"

"I think he said two o'clock."

Twenty-nine

Hickey and Greenie stayed to watch me open the envelope. I told them to go away and make out or something, but they just sat on the sofa and waited.

"Who do you think it's from?" Greenie asked.

"No *le* clue," I lied.

We were all surprised, though, when I broke the seal with a steak knife and found a bundle of twenty-dollar bills with their edges all soft and torn.

"Are you selling drugs?" Hickey asked. He seemed hopeful.

"Hickey!" Greenie said, smacking him. "Are you?" she asked.

"Not that I know of," I said.

"Count it," Hickey said.

I was concentrating pretty hard on hiding from them a torn piece of paper that was tucked down in front of the sheaf of bills. I wanted desperately to read it but just as desperately to prevent Hickey and Greenie from knowing anything at all about Amiel de la Cruz. I began to count the money just so that I could hide the torn piece of paper.

"It's two hundred and forty dollars," I said.

"Why is somebody giving you two hundred and forty dollars?" Greenie asked.

"More like totally *failing* to give it to you," Hickey said.

"I don't know," I lied. The amount of Amiel's medical bill was $240.

"If you think it's some mistake, and it's really for that other Pearl, the drug dealer of La Santa Margarita," Hickey said, "I can keep the money for you." He did a pretty good Spanish accent, which annoyed me.

"I'd better ask my uncle about it," I said. This made no sense, so I had to keep improvising as I talked. "He pays the workers in cash, see, and maybe one of them dropped it."

Hickey and Greenie stared at me. "In an envelope with your name on it?"

"Well," I said, "sometimes my uncle *loans* money, too, and maybe somebody was paying him back."

"Again," Hickey said slowly, "I have to point out the weirdness of putting your name on the envelope. Are you, like, your uncle's cashier?"

This was a terrific idea, and I seized it. "Yes, actually. I am. He's thinking of making me a part-time secretary. I balance his checkbook and whatnot." *Whatnot?* I had just used the word *whatnot.*

"But do the guys who pick your uncle's avocados go, you know, recreational hiking a lot?" Greenie asked.

"No, I don't think so," I said. "But they fish and stuff." I had actually seen some Hispanic guys at the river once with professional-looking nets. I remember wondering what in the world they might catch.

"They do?" Greenie asked. "Weird."

"Why is that weird?"

"I don't know. It just seems kind of *wildernessy*. The few times my dad's had a Mexican help him with yard work, the guy brought those cup-o'-noodle things."

"Some of them are different," I said.

"Yeah," Hickey said, getting suddenly animated. "Some of them are totally living in the wild here. Remember that story a while back in the newspaper?"

I shook my head. I was holding the envelope closed and wishing they would go away so I could read the note. I wondered if Amiel realized that he'd dropped the cash and was looking frantically for it all over the trail.

"A bunch of migrants were living in a canyon over in Carlsbad, I think it was," Hickey went on. "And there were these places in the reeds where they would go and meet prostitutes. The reason it was in the paper was one of the women was told she'd have a good job when she came over to the U.S., and she could earn back the money to pay the coyote who brought her across. But then she found out she had to work in one of those reed brothels."

"That's disgusting," Greenie said.

"Yeah," Hickey said. "I wouldn't be surprised if there's a place like that in Fallbrook."

"I've never seen anything remotely like that," I said numbly. "Anyway, thanks for bringing this. You could have just kept it, obviously." On impulse, I reached into the envelope and pulled out a twenty. "Here," I said. "You should get a reward. I'll replace the money when I give it to my uncle."

"No way," Hickey said, standing up and looking insulted. "No. I don't need a reward to give people their own stuff back. If you don't find the owner, though, you can buy us all a Pedro's."

Greenie stood up, too, and they made their way out of the living room, onto the porch, and into the sun.

Thirty

I fished out a little shred of paper, its shape as irregular as Illinois, and read,

Please give this money to Mrs. Agnese.
Thank you from Amiel.

I was freakishly disappointed. The bundle of cash might have made it unlikely that I would find a passionate letter that began, *Fly to me, mi amor,* but he could have said something a *little* more personal.

Then again, wouldn't it have been more direct—and easier—for Amiel to knock on the door and give the money to my aunt? Or my uncle? Why involve me at all?

I heard a car door shut, and in a few minutes, my mother came scuffling through the avocado grove. Leaf-scuffling can be fun when you're in a good mood, as long as you forget to worry that you'll scuffle over a rattlesnake, but my mother looked as if she'd welcome a fatal snakebite. I stuffed the money and the note under a sofa cushion and went to meet her on the porch.

"Mrs. Bookseller, I presume?" I asked, trying to be chipper for her.

My mother didn't look happy when she said she didn't know yet.

"Was the interviewer nice?" I went on in a peppy tone. Somehow our roles were upside down, like our old house. Normally, the teenage girl dresses in a sensible skirt and goes to job interviews and the mother asks if the interviewer was nice.

"Kind of patronizing," she said stiffly, tossing her purse on the chair. I could tell by the way she avoided my eyes that she wanted me to clam up. Go *away*, she was thinking. *Leave me alone*.

Once you're upside down, though, it's hard to revolve back to the right position. If I weren't peppy, who would be? What would happen to us?

"Want me to make you Breakfast in a Barrel?" I asked. Breakfast in a Barrel was the egg-and-potato burrito we'd eaten every morning on a family vacation in Hawaii and then adopted as a dinner dish.

"I already ate," she said. She didn't sit, and she didn't go to the computer to check e-mail. The only people she heard from anymore were attorneys, so who could blame her? "Thanks," she added.

"I'm going for a walk," I said. I waited a little too long before I asked, "Wanna come with me?"

I'm sorry to say that I was glad when she shook her head, glad when she said she was going to take a nap and then maybe check out some more job listings. "Okay," I said, relief insulating me from her. It was the same stuff that deafened and padded me when I stood there and watched her scream insults at my father in the dark avocado grove. She needed saving, but I didn't move. It was as if my mother, the expert swimmer, were drowning, but I had never learned to swim.

"Okay," I said again, and watched her go to her bedroom, take off my homecoming dance heels, and lie down fully clothed on her unmade bed.

Thirty-one

I waited until she was asleep before I slipped the money back out from under the cushion and made for my bicycle, taking a roundabout way to see if there were still loquats on the tree.

Loquats taste like tiny peaches dipped in lemonade. They're kind of like the manna God dropped every day for the Israelites: delicious if you eat them right away, but if you try to put them in a bowl for the next day, they go brown and wrinkly. It's best to eat them outside so you can peel the skin off with your teeth, then bite the globe in two so you can examine and remove the cluster of two or three slippery brown seeds. These you also have to throw out, but it's fun to look at them first, all puzzled up together and wet like something from a tide pool. I once ate twenty-two loquats without being sick. On this occasion, I ate three or four, then snapped off a whole branch and tucked it carefully into my backpack for a picnic at the river.

I found Amiel where tall, skinny oaks and sycamores bend toward each other like a cathedral over Agua Prieta Creek. The path curved sharply to the north ahead of me, deep inside the arched bower of trees, and I saw him when he was just fifty yards away, a dark-haired boy wearing a red plaid shirt, his head down as he scanned the ground for something.

Because he was so busy looking down, I had three or four seconds to think of what to do, and sometimes when you have time to think of what to do, you see what a ninny you are. I stopped walking. I sat down on a fallen log. I faced away from the trail and pretended, like a ninny, that I was completely unaware of him. I thought my act of obliviousness would be more realistic if I had some reason to be sitting down, so I opened my backpack and brought out—presto, chango—the branch of loquats. I snapped off one, peeled it, bit it in half, and pretended to examine the glossy brown seeds. I could hear footsteps, so I knew Amiel saw me, but I didn't turn my head. I ate the other half of the loquat, and then I dropped the interlocking seeds.

The footsteps stopped. I could feel that he was near me, and I still couldn't speak. I reached into my backpack, felt for the envelope all thick with money, and pulled it out. I held it out to him and then, only then, did I have the courage to look at his face.

There are emotions your face can't hide, and he was intensely relieved. His bandaged hand, worn leather work boots, and black eyebrows—all the heavy parts of him—appeared to become weightless, the way your arms do when you've pressed them hard against a doorway and then stepped away to let them float all by themselves. Greenie and I used to make our arms float all the time, going from doorway to doorway in her house.

Amiel looked at the envelope for a few seconds, and I waited for him to speak. He smiled instead, showing the white tiles of his teeth.

"A friend of mine found it," I said. "Isn't that weird?"

All around us the just-born leaves of the sycamores brushed against each other in a wind that was blowing from the north. It was hot like the Santa Anas, and it would burn clouds away like a welder's torch and bake the new leaves into card stock.

Amiel looked up at the sycamores, where the limbs were mottled white and gray and the huge green leaves, nine inches across, touched gently together. I looked at his hands, one swollen and wrapped, one narrow and finely made, and I held out a loquat. He took one and bit into it, and I took another one, and we ate them without a word in the shadows.

This is the most beautiful place, I thought but didn't say. *I feel the strangest happiness.* The words weren't specific enough somehow. I didn't have words for what I felt.

Maybe that's why, now that Amiel's gone, I trace and label the parts of the sycamore in my college botany classes: *pistillate flowers, rounded sepals, acute petals.*

"You dropped the envelope, I guess," I said.

Amiel nodded.

"What do you call it again—*hacer mal . . .*" I couldn't

remember how to say "juggle." I tossed one loquat to the other hand.

"*Hacer malabares,*" he whispered. He couldn't juggle with his hand in a bandage, and we couldn't talk, so what I felt—the strange happiness, the nearness of him—just got larger and had nowhere to go, as when the sycamore tree swells and strains against heavy bark.

The rigid texture of sycamore bark entirely lacks the expansive power common to the bark of other trees, so it is incapable of stretching to accommodate the growth of the wood underneath, and the tree sloughs it off in great irregular masses, leaving the surface mottled, greenish white and gray.

Amiel handed the envelope back to me. "*Sí,*" he said, lifting his hurt hand slightly. He tried to curve it into the letter C.

"She won't take it, you know," I said. "My aunt."

He nodded very slowly and intensely at me. "*Sí,*" he said again.

I'm not good at arguing with people. I took the envelope and put it in my backpack. All the greenness around us fluttered in the wind, and I was afraid he would go away, but he didn't leave me, and he didn't speak. I suppose I couldn't stand it any longer, the silence and the nearness of his hand to my own skin, which like sycamore bark entirely lacked expansive power. I turned my face with the intention of speaking, and he turned his face to mine with the intention of hearing. I had nothing adequate to say, he had nothing to hear, and so we left our faces in that position of mute expectation. His cheeks were flat and long and smooth, hollowed by something that was now gone, like the interlocking loquat seeds. On one cheek, he had a little scar like those craters on photos of the moon. His eyes were both still and not still. His lips were dry, and I felt them near to mine the way you can feel a fever before you touch a sick person's skin. I couldn't say if he moved forward slightly or if I moved my face, but we did move, and our lips touched. He smelled like dust and loquats. I would have stayed forever in that moment, but he broke away. His face was darker and more melancholy than before—angry, even.

"Sorry," I said, my first impulse being to apologize.

He looked around us. I knew what he was looking for: witnesses to our kiss. The chest-cracking swells went on inside me. The trees were just the same in their posture, blind to us, invisibly growing inside that stiff bark. The brown seeds we'd spit out lay all around us, dirty now. I thought of saying, *It isn't wrong. Why is it wrong?*

It wasn't wrong in theory. It wasn't forbidden. But I understood that it was very strange and different, someone like him and someone like me. The people who have nothing aren't allowed to touch the people with cars and houses. They can work here. That's all.

I could hear the leaves patting each other in the wind, and I tried to hear the water in the creek, but it made no sound as it drained and pooled and crept and slid. Amiel didn't run away from me, but he stood forbiddingly still. I looked at his furious eyebrows and his mouth and the shoulders that inside the red plaid shirt were strong from picking and climbing and digging and hauling.

"This is America," I said. "Right? In America, we're the same. Equal."

He didn't answer me.

I considered the other reasons a boy might break away from kissing me, such as my weird eyeballs and lack of Greenie-size boobs. "What is it?" I asked him in a miserable voice, one that made me feel and sound like a kid who's about to cry.

He stood like one of those Olympic gymnasts before a vault. He shook his head without letting me see his eyes.

I waited. I didn't say, "Why not?" because I didn't want to hear that the reason was not being attracted to me.

He turned then and walked back along the path the way he had come, and I had no choice but to go my own way home.

Thirty-two

This is what happened when I took the money to my aunt Agnès. I waited until Robby wasn't home, of course. I found her standing at the kitchen island opening the mail while Robby's dog, Snowy, nibbled dry food out of his red dish. Snowy sniffed at my shoes, then went back to nibbling.

"Amiel wanted me to give you this," I said, and I set the stack of bills on the granite beside a glossy French magazine. The money looked frazzled and worn, as if it was too shabby to belong to her.

"What?" she asked. She wore a white ribbed sweater with short sleeves and a long necklace of pink stones that clicked when she moved. She was still studying a bill that she'd sliced open with a dashing silver letter opener. Every surface in the room—the granite, her oval fingernails, her short dark hair, the glasses in the cupboard—gleamed.

"Amiel wants to pay you back," I said. "For the doctor."

She wrinkled her perfect forehead and her sculpted mouth. *"Pourquoi?"* she asked. "He is our responsibility."

"I guess he didn't like being dependent," I said, knowing also that he'd hurt himself juggling, which wasn't her responsibility at all.

She adjusted the handle of her porcelain teacup, out of which steam curled gracefully. My aunt was a fan of fruit teas without sugar, and I thought I could smell sour pomegranate peel.

"Why did he give it to *you?*" she asked, her focus now changing in the way I'd feared it would.

I blushed, and she took a sip of her sour tea. "Do you want?" she asked, indicating the tea. I shook my head, and her look changed to sober consideration of me. "Where do you see him?" she asked.

"I don't see him. Except for this. I ran into him, and he made me promise to give it to you."

"Ah," my aunt said. "I am not believing you."

Snowy scrabbled in his dish.

"It's true, though," I said. "There is absolutely *nothing* between us." I said it with enough misery in my face, I suppose, that she believed me. "I have to go," I said.

"Come back later," she said sympathetically, holding her thin teacup aloft but not taking a sip. "You and your mother should come for dinner now that you won't have so much school. Come tonight."

"Thank you," I said, "but my mom already started something. It was in the Crock-Pot when I left."

This wasn't true, but it worked. When I left, the worn money was on the counter and my aunt was telling me that I was a very beautiful girl and I should let her take me shopping when school let out.

Thirty-three

I took exams and signed yearbooks and cleaned out my locker without another call from my father, my mother began working at the bookstore, and a single moth emerged from the nest of cocoons on my mother's desk. The moth was white and ladylike and so still she might have been a pair of flower petals on a thick, furry stem. Although we checked every morning and every afternoon, anxiously expecting her mate, the other cocoons stayed whole and motionless. If you held one of them to the light, you could see a dark shape inside. The lady moth in her white dress waited a whole week, and then, as if she'd reached some final hour, she began to lay sterile eggs all over the nearest cocoons, embossing them with yellow unfertilized seeds. Then, imperceptibly, she died. Nothing changed about her appearance, but if you nudged her, you could tell she was gone.

"What are you going to do with her now?" I asked my mother.

"I don't know," my mother said. "I'm thinking."

When my mother left for work, I went to the river. It didn't belong to Amiel, I reasoned, and I found certain places on other banks where I felt completely alone. I read books I'd been meaning to read and books I'd read before. I ate peanut-butter-and-banana sandwiches and Corn Pops, but no more loquats. I took close-up photographs of the water, the bark, dead leaves, a molted lizard, and a dogface butterfly. I drew pictures of insects in a notebook and tried to identify them the way we'd been required to do in eighth grade, when I was forced to push pins through the bodies of beetles my father helped me catch with a Smucker's jar full of poison. I drew pictures of plants, too, and this is how I learned to tell miner's lettuce from black sage, virgin's bower, and snakeweed. For the rest of June, the weather was mostly foggy and white, as still as the dead cocoons. Then July came and the sun burned yellow flowers called butter and eggs into brown straw, the dodder crept like orange Silly String over the poison ivy, and an insect I never saw made a continuous, furious ticking sound.

I don't know how often Amiel watched me. In the daytime, I assumed he was away at work, but in the evenings or late afternoons, the whole canyon felt like a tunnel waiting for a train. I listened for him with my feet and my spine and my averted head, but to the hikers who cracked by with their sniffing, leaping dogs, it was just me and my Brontë book, me and my *Pocket Field Guide,* me and my Corn Pops. I was the hobo girl of Agua Prieta.

Greenie didn't miss me because she and Hickey had entered a cocoon of their own. They were always together, and Hickey plainly didn't want me there. Robby, too, had his preoccupations: a college prep class in Claremont that met five days a week for the first four weeks of summer, then a music camp slightly less prestigious than the one he'd failed to try out for in April. My father neither called nor wrote to ask if I'd changed my mind about Paris. My whole life reminded me of how it felt to ride, when Greenie and I were little, in the back of Greenie's mother's car, an ancient Pacer with a seat that faced backward and left us staring at places we'd already been and drivers who didn't want to make eye contact. I was facing the wrong direction, but time still went forward, gliding toward destinations I couldn't see or choose.

One week my mother decided to have it out with the cocoons. She followed directions from a guy who had his own silk business, and the first, most disgusting step was to extract the worms. Out they came, dead and yellow. Then she soaked the cocoons in hot water. She mushed them around, expecting the hard glue to just melt away, but soon she had a bunch of dented egg shapes that reminded me of Ping-Pong balls you've run over with a car. Still, she dried them in the sun, and the next day, right after breakfast, she picked at one until she'd teased out a strand of silk. One strand after another came off in her hands like foot-long hanks of spiderweb. I kept expecting her to give up, but she wrapped the webby bits around and around until she had a miniature ball of truly unimpressive silk. One down, eight to go.

"Now what?" I said.

My mother dumped the rest of the mashed, hollow cocoons in the kitchen trash, and the lid came down with a clap. She set the tiny ball of silk in the basket of random objects she kept on her desk. She took the corpse of the lady moth outside and set her on a gardenia bush. Then she came back inside.

"Sometimes," she said slowly, as if she were still searching for a useful moral, "you've got to know when to give up."

She left for work, and I hiked all the way to a series of boulders the size of cars that caused the river to flow fast and loud around them. You could stretch out your whole body on some of those rocks, but they were also prime real estate for taggers, who left giant black graffiti names like FZZZJ or PVVR! It was hot, though, really hot, and the coldest water swirled through those little rapids. I was wearing my swimsuit under my clothes, a one-piece from last summer that I'd never really liked. I soaked my hair and my face, and then I let the current push me to a shallow pool where I closed my eyes and pretended I was a piece of moss, hands on the grainy shore, legs floating free. I looked around, as I floated, for shells to add to my collection. There's only one kind of shell at the river, a clam the color of Wite-Out that I like to rub with my thumb when I'm reading, and I'd been taking them home in my pockets and adding them to a jar I kept in Robby's tree house.

When I came back to the rock, my book was still there. So

was my dad's old backpack. Nothing looked any different until I opened my paperback copy of *Wuthering Heights* and found, neatly folded like a bookmark, a piece of lined notebook paper.

On the outside was a drawing of an open oyster shell holding a pearl. I unfolded it and shivered. *GO TO BLACK OAK*, it said. I did a full-circle survey of the surrounding trees, heart pounding, but I didn't see Amiel. I tugged my shirt and shorts back on over my wet swimsuit and walked to the only place I thought might be the black oak, a huge tree burned to volcanic rock by a fire a long time ago. It was hollow on the inside, so it made me think of elves and dwarves and leprechauns whenever I passed it. It now held a red bandanna tied to form a little bag. The bundle clacked when I opened the knot, and dozens of white shells spilled over the ground.

Carefully, I turned them all over.

"Olly olly in come free," I said when I stood up, as if Amiel knew the rules of the game.

Nothing and no one.

"That means you can come out!" I said.

Someone brushed against a tree, but when I turned, it was just a hiker with a spaniel on a leash. "Hide-and-seek?" she asked.

"Yes," I said.

"Maybe my Greta will sniff 'em out," she said, and went striding along with Greta while I picked up my white shells and put them carefully back into the bandanna.

I looked everywhere as I walked back along the trail—up in the trees, down the eroded banks where roots tangled with stones and cobwebs, along the sandbars glittering in the sun. Finally I came to the crossing point. Amiel's shore, as I thought of it. All I had to do was wade across to the grotto. Perhaps he was in there, his back to the wall, listening and waiting as I used to wait in my favorite hiding place at Greenie's house, a warm spot between the propane tank and a pink hibiscus. It was that memory that coaxed me to remove my shoes and slosh over, to step with a hammering heart to the wall that was warm and slivery under my touch. I knew Amiel was too skilled at hiding not to hear my approach. I made myself count to ten, and then I sprang into his doorway.

No one.

"Amiel?" I said. All seemed to be in order, though I couldn't be sure because the room was dark. I stepped in and heard a small sound, no louder than the frisking of a bird or a lizard in dry leaves. I turned around and there he was, seated on the floor beside the wall, waiting for me to spot him. He smiled the way you do when you're glad to be found.

"You're supposed to run now," I said.

He shrugged and stayed where he was.

"Or you're going to be it."

I had no idea whether they played hide-and-seek in Mexico. Still, it was a game that let me be confident instead of self-conscious and confused, so I reached out my hand to touch the nearest part of him, which was his knee. "Tag," I said. "You're it."

If he had run, I could have chased him and known what I was doing, because I know how to be eight, nine, ten, and eleven, but he stood up and looked as confused as I felt. He was holding a long, smooth stick in one hand and a knife that he folded and put in his pocket.

"Thank you," I said, holding up the bandanna. "For the shells."

He nodded.

He was two inches from me, and I could see the black stone disk between his collar bones rising and falling with his breath, so I found it hard to think. I wondered again how he bathed in the river because he smelled and looked clean, but the thought of him swimming naked in the river made my breathing more shallow still. I tried to focus on something other than his body, and what I found was the green and black tin box that I'd shamelessly opened on my first visit, the one with the old-fashioned lords and ladies on the outside. I picked it up and said, lamely, that it was pretty.

Amiel nodded and when I set the tin down, he picked it back up and tapped the photograph into his hand. He held it for me and pointed at the little boy, then at himself.

"Is that your mother?" I asked.

He nodded, so I asked if that was his house, and he nodded again.

"Do you write to her?" I asked.

He shook his head.

"May I sit down?" I asked.

This time, he didn't immediately answer me with a nod or a shake. He leaned briefly against the wall, but then he offered me a kind of tree stump and went outside. I sat on the tree stump and waited, listening hard for clues to where he'd gone. I stared at the bags of ramen noodles and a can of black beans and wished I'd brought loquats again.

Amiel returned with another log roughly the same size and set it down. Our knees were almost but not quite touching, and I felt the way the sea looks in the afternoon, when every wave glows.

"How long ago did you first come here?" I asked.

He drew in the dirt with the stick that looked like it had been whittled smooth and then charred in a fire. He wrote the numeral four.

For some reason, the way he was writing in the dirt reminded me of the way Greenie and I would talk to each other in church. For a while, her family took me with them to services and during the long sermons we would write on each other's backs with a fingertip and the other person would try to guess the word.

"Where do you cook?" I asked.

He seemed glad to stand up and go somewhere else. I followed him out to a path that led through willows so thick and low that you'd think it wasn't worth it to swat your way through. Then we came to a huge mangled sycamore growing half under and half over a hollowed-out bank. The roots formed a sort of ladder that he climbed, reaching down to give me his hand at the top.

Once I stopped feeling the terrific buzz of his hand on mine, I could look around. We were standing on a strange little plateau where someone had once built a little house out of river rock and stucco. The house still had a doorway but no door, four windows but no glass, a chimney but no roof, and a concrete floor. All around the ruined house the trees were near enough and tall enough so that they formed a sort of blind, and I thought you probably couldn't see it at all from nearby hills.

Inside the house, near the hearth, Amiel had built a sort of fire pit with rocks. It was a safer place to cook than most camp-sites, really, because there was concrete all around, and I longed to be there when he had a fire going, when we could be cowgirl and cowboy and pretend we weren't a few miles from two million people. We stood in the sunlit, roofless house and looked down at the charred rocks.

"I love it here," I said.

Amiel poked at the coals with the stick he'd used to write on the dirt floor of his other house. His sore hand had only a small bandage on it and I reached out to touch it.

"It's better, I guess?" I said.

Amiel wrote *SI* with the black end of the stick, each stroke reminding me of the skin-writing game with Greenie.

"Good," I said.

He balanced the stick on one palm while standing still and then while walking in a circle. He tossed it so that it whirled several times in the air, then caught it.

"Let me try," I said. He handed me the stick, and I balanced it for a few seconds on my palm. I tried again, chasing after it as it wobbled and fell. Everything seemed perfect. "Can I come back here?"

His face was unsettled.

"Give me your hand," I said in a teasing voice, and he held out his flat palm as if waiting for me to balance the stick there, but I left the stick where it fell and pulled on his arm until it was outstretched. I felt him tremble a little as I wrote with my finger in the palm of his hand, P. Then, on his wrist and forearm, I wrote the rest of the word, PLEASE.

When Greenie and I played the game, we almost never managed to guess each other's words. Letters, yes, but long words took repetition. Amiel closed his hand over the letter P on my second try and withdrew his arm. Then he turned around and faced the empty walls of the ruined house. He crouched down in front of the dead fire and poked at the crumbs of black wood. He refused to look at me, and he shook his head.

I had nothing else to say or do, so I turned and walked through the doorless door of the roofless house, and when I had picked my way down the root-twisted bank, I couldn't wait for the open trail so that I could run and run and run.

Thirty-four

A few days later, I resumed my old habits of reading and swimming, but I stayed away from Amiel's part of the river. The days were pale green and flat, like water that got stuck in the reeds and went nowhere. I could have opened my eyes underwater and seen my life as a sunken object, floating and trapped, green with algae.

I was so used to my stagnation that when I found another note from him that said BLACK OAK, I went as far as the tree, picked up the small dark-blue bottle with a white flower poking out of the top, and then just put it in my backpack. I didn't go looking for Amiel because whatever we were doing, it wasn't hide-and-seek. Twice more he left notes and twice more I followed them. I collected the pair of acorns joined like the chambers of a heart. The small papery man made from cornhusks. I set them all with the jar of shells on the windowsill of

Robby's tree house, where, I figured, my mother wouldn't see them but Amiel, who still worked in my uncle's grove on Fridays, might walk through the grove and see the silent progress of his gifts.

It was mid-July when my mother's friend Louise asked my mother, "What's Pearl doing on Mission Road without a helmet?"

By this point, my mother was so thin she could wear things from the junior department at Macy's, and she wore brighter lipstick. Between her eyebrows were two wrinkles I'd recently learned (from reading the type of magazine she never used to buy, but now, confusingly, did) were called the "11." When she was angry with me, the lines deepened. I watched them go dark as she said, "Where in the world have you been going?"

"Just the river," I said.

"With Greenie?"

"No."

"I already told you it isn't safe for you to be there alone, and it isn't safe to ride your bike on Mission Road."

"The migrants do it."

Occasionally, you saw muscled men in helmets, sunglasses, and Spandex using the bike lanes of Fallbrook, but mostly it was dark-skinned men in ball caps.

"They," my mother said, "have no *choice*."

"What else am I going to do all day?"

"If you're going to ride your bike like a migrant, you can get a job like a migrant."

"So it's safe to ride on Mission if I have a job."

My mother blinked. She twisted an earring. "Not safe. Just defensible. And you have to wear a helmet."

"Fine," I said.

So the following morning, while my mother watched, I put on a hideous old helmet that used to be Robby's. I told her when I would be home and exactly where I was going to fill out applications: Major Market and Subway. But after I left those places, I stopped, on a whim, at the Cup o' Europe, which was right across the alley from the fake Irish pub and had a WE'RE HIRING sign in the window.

The manager, Chloe, was this big friendly woman with a cold, and she was just being polite, I could tell, in letting me apply for the job at all (PREVIOUS EXPERIENCE PREFERRED, the sign said in smaller letters), but as she was reading the top line of my application, she said, "Are you related to Sharon DeWitt?"

My thigh muscles felt like ironing boards. "Yes," I said.

"As in?"

"She's my mother."

"Well, that would be odd," she said, letting out an overly big laugh. "Do you two bicker?"

"Not usually," I said, shrugging.

"You could work together?"

"I guess so. Why?"

Another overly big laugh. "You know she works here, right?"

I felt my neck prickle and wondered how many of the people sitting on the big comfy sofas and big comfy chairs were listening in on our conversation while pretending to work on their laptops. As far as I could tell, the Cup o' Europe was not a bookstore. There were some used books in the back, where a sign said, LEAVE ONE, TAKE ONE!! but most of them were large print. Also, the two girls working the coffee machines were teenagers, not grown women like my mother.

"What a coincidence!" I said, trying to work up a laugh. It seemed really, really strange that no one I knew, such as Greenie, had mentioned my mother's new job at Cup o' Europe. During the school year, I would have heard about my mom's job from seven people within ten minutes of her first shift. But since school let out, I'd stopped speaking to practically everyone.

"I guess you two need to *talk* more, huh?" Chloe the manager said. "I'll bet you're like my kids. Always rushing off to do whatsit with whosit."

"Pretty much," I said. "Ha!" I paused because it's hard to follow up a fake laugh. "Probably we shouldn't work together, actually," I said.

"You'd want different shifts?"

"No. I think I should just, you know, *withdraw*. Don't tell her I was here, even."

But of course Chloe told her. The next night during our soup course (the only course), my mother set down her twisted shred of a napkin and said, "Chloe said you came by."

"You said you worked in a bookstore," I said.

"They sell books. After a fashion."

"I don't know why you had to put it that way to me is all."

189

"I think they're planning to sell books. That's what they told me when I applied, anyway."

I blinked at her, and she picked up the remote. We watched anchormen, crime tape, the fuzzy progress of car chases, and finally, for comic relief, a tour of the thing I had thought existed only in my imagination: a house that was literally upside down. A man in Poland had painstakingly wedged the pitched roof of a house into the ground and built the rest of the house up from there, balancing the weight somehow on the point of the triangle. The foundation was high and flat like a tray held up by a waiter. On the edge of this elevated foundation, a little cypress tree grew (or merely pointed) straight down.

"The house took twice as long to build as an ordinary structure," said the newscaster, "because being inside the house made the workers dizzy."

Long lines of curious families waited outside the house for a tour. "Some people have waited as long as six hours to see the inside," the newscaster announced as Poles and Germans, looking just like Americans in their baby carriers, Windbreakers, T-shirts, and track shoes, traipsed unsteadily through upside-down doorways to run their hands along upside-down beds. I began, sitting there beside my lost and lonely mother, to plan my pilgrimage to this place where I would finally be at home.

Thirty-five

The next day, Subway called to say I was hired, which meant long bike rides, no time to sink myself down in the river, and the persistent smell of mustard on my skin. Twice that week I got phone messages from my father, but they didn't mention his condo or Paris or plans of any kind to see me, so I didn't call him back.

I rode home that Friday at five o'clock, long after Amiel would have gone home. The grove felt empty, and I knew the guesthouse would be empty, too, because it was open-mike night at the Cup o' Europe, a shift my mother was unhappy to take. I was halfway up the porch steps when I saw something small and dark beside the screen door: Amiel's tin box. The black enamel felt so warm from the sun that it almost burned me when I picked it up.

I sat on the porch in case he was out there somewhere,

watching me, and I pried open the lid. I could hear crows calling and lizards rattling through the dried bougainvillea blossoms and eucalyptus bark. "Is that you?" I called hopefully, not daring to say Amiel's name in case my aunt was outside. A lizard blinked at me from under a curled leaf and did a couple of push-ups to show me he had the situation under control.

The tin held a small, flat piece of wood. On one side, in charcoal, it said only,

Sí.

I held the wood in my palm and considered the crow poking through the avocado leaves for food. My last question to Amiel had been, *Can I come back here?*

And now I had his answer in my hand, sharper than a Scrabble tile.

Sí.

Thirty-six

I tried conversation, of course. I'd never spent time with anyone who was so quiet. When Amiel took me fishing, I said, "What kind of fish is it?"

He shrugged.

"I guess you wouldn't know the American names." I watched the water reflect the sky. I watched the dragonflies buzz the reeds. But I could only keep still for about two minutes before a question rose to the surface like a swimmer up for air. "Do you think they're native?"

He shrugged. Again, how would he know? It went on like that until finally he pointed to the water, raised his left eyebrow, and whispered, "*Silencio.*"

"I love it when you speak the Espanish," I whispered back.

He rolled his eyes because I wasn't being quiet, so I sat still and didn't say a word until, forty or fifty years later, we had a big flapping fish on the line. "Woo-hoo!" is what I said then, and he had to give me the *silencio* sign again.

"What?" I said. "We've got it now."

He pointed to the other side of the river, where the trail cut through the trees.

"Oh," I said. True. We didn't want other hikers to notice us.

Next we went to gut the fish. He had me dig a hole with a sharp, flat rock he brought out from its hiding place. Then he started to cut the fish, and I started to look away. I was studying the tree limbs in order to keep my mind off the vomit impulse when I asked him how he got to the United States.

He was wiping his hands by then. *"Caminando,"* he said, and he made his fingers walk like little legs.

"But how did you know which way to go? Did you have a coyote?" I knew that's what newspapers called the smugglers who brought illegals across, but I didn't know what Amiel was likely to call them.

In any case, he didn't answer. He made me bury the guts, and then he took the edible parts of the fish in a piece of newspaper up to the fire pit in the old stone house. It was six o'clock on a Monday, and the gnats glowed like fireflies. I could hear a rooster and a dove, both cheerful sounds. I did some sweeping with a little broom I'd brought and Amiel built the fire.

"So you didn't tell me how you got here," I said once I'd done my sweeping. "Or about your childhood. Like how you learned to do circus stuff. Or the accident when you hurt your throat."

I sat cross-legged beside him and he fed little bits of dry bark to his fire.

Without a word, he poked at the fire until it was big enough to ignite sticks. He set an array of firewood on the coals, and then his hands were empty.

"I'd just like to know about you," I said.

Amiel took my hand, and at that moment, the doves seemed to be making their sound just for me. He drew the shape of a 2 in my palm, and when I read the number aloud, he whispered, "Long."

"Too long," I said. It was like texting for early man, and I wanted to do it some more.

Amiel just nodded and looked at the fire.

"If it's long, you could tell me a little at a time," I said.

He kept holding my hand and watching the fire, and we were happy.

Thirty-seven

August came. At work, I wore flat, baggy, plastic gloves to layer meat and vegetables on sandwiches that were too often for people I knew at school, who always thought I owed them free extra portions of bacon and avocado. I don't know if my father was in Paris, but Robby was. Robby always spent most of August there with my uncle, my aunt Agnès, his *grandmère*, and Monsieur Pouf the tortoise, whom I imagined on a leash held by Robby, scraping its slow way past the Eiffel Tower.

Robby and I had barely spoken all summer, but he sent me a postcard of Tintin and Snowy. *Bonjour le you*, he wrote. *France is le bon. Plan going très bien so far. Will parlez-vous when we get back. Robby.*

I didn't know what the plan was, unless it was the one where he went on dating someone he didn't respect, but the next day, I had a surprise customer at Subway.

"I'd like a turkey on whole wheat, please," Mary Beth said, and I said what I'm supposed to say, which is, "Do you want that toasted?" Then I couldn't help looking shocked to see her.

She asked if I was going on break soon, which unfortunately I was, and that's how I came to be sitting in a booth with her as she unwrapped her sandwich.

"You look tan," I said. "Been playing a lot of tennis?"

"I have, actually," she said. "I need the money, so I've been teaching more lessons."

I said that sounded nice.

"Mrs. Wallace went to Paris, though, so she's not taking lessons right now."

This was a new twist. "I didn't know you were teaching her," I said.

"Yeah, that's how I first met the Wallaces," Mary Beth said. "Agnès was looking for someone to help her brush up on her game, and the regular coach at the club recommended me."

This all seemed logical. I decided to ask if my uncle took lessons, too.

"No," she said. She looked away and fiddled with the wrapper of her sandwich. She ate a stray piece of lettuce.

"Did I do something wrong with your sandwich?" I asked.

"No," she said. "I just don't feel that hungry. Do you want it?"

"That's okay," I said, though I did. I hadn't eaten yet.

"Are you sure?"

"Yes."

Finally, after a long, uncomfortable pause, Mary Beth said, "I came here because I wondered if Robby said anything to you."

"About what?"

"About me."

"I've barely spoken to him," I said, not wanting to look straight at her. "First he was at these college prep camps and music camp, and now he's in Paris with my aunt and uncle."

"I know," she said.

"Oh," I said, confused. "So did you two go out this summer or not?"

"When he was home, we did," she said. "And I drove up to Orange County once when he was doing that music camp and we met for dinner."

That seemed kind of serious. "To tell you the truth," I said, "he's never gone out with girls much. He's always kind of focused on school and track and music."

"Yeah, he told me that," she said. "He said I was the only person he'd ever wanted to date."

That seemed misleading at best, given what the reasons for his interest had been.

"And now he's just completely stopped calling me."

"It's probably expensive," I said.

"And e-mailing me," she said.

"Well, I haven't gotten any e-mail from him, either. I don't know what the setup is at his grandmother's. She's kind of old and she might not be wired for that kind of thing."

"I've been to Europe," she said. "There's an Internet café on every corner."

"Well," I said, out of excuses, "I just wouldn't wait around for him. He's really fickle lately. He's not even as friendly with me as we used to be." I wanted to add, *Besides, he's just a high school student*, but to point out that he was beneath her seemed insulting to both of them.

She sighed and looked truly miserable. "Okay," she said. "Thanks for talking to me about it. I realize he's too young for me, but he doesn't seem young. And I just thought there might be some reason why he went from sixty miles an hour to a dead stop, you know? I just don't get why he'd be so intense about it and then, for no apparent reason, just shut off."

"I don't know, either," I said, and reminded myself that Mary Beth had engaged in some sort of romance with my married uncle and was not deserving of sympathy. I told myself not to eat her sandwich, either, even though my break was nearly over.

"Are you sure he didn't say anything else to you?" Mary Beth asked. "He didn't say, for instance, that he was going to stop dating me because . . ." She waited for me to fill in the blank.

I tried to formulate an answer in my mind as she wrapped the sandwich back up. It crossed my mind to say, *He saw you kissing my uncle*. Or, *He wanted to stop you from breaking up his parents' marriage*. I should have said these things, I think now, but I didn't, which made me wonder if I was losing my compulsive honesty now that I spent most of my time leading a secret life.

"No," I said to Mary Beth. "He didn't."

"Okay," she said. "Thanks, anyway," and, taking the sandwich that she didn't want, she walked away from me, and as I'd feared she would, she dropped it in the trash.

Thirty-eight

I told my mother I had more shifts at Subway than I really did so I could be at the river when I wasn't at work, waiting for Amiel to draw letters on the trembling skin of my palm. More often, though, he wrote what he had to say on the dirt or answered me, if the weather wasn't too hot and dry, in his raspy voice.

I would ask a question: "So where were you born?"

It took a while to spell out *San Ygnacio, Guanajuato*.

Another time, I asked about his father.

Estados Unidos, he wrote.

"But where? Here?"

The answer was too long to write, so he whispered, "My father sent my mother money until I had four years, but then he stopped."

"Why?"

Amiel shrugged.

"What happened to your mother?"

With the stick he drew what looked like a small hill, and then he drew a cross on top of it.

The day I finally spotted the green string hammock wadded up in the willows and brought it to him, he untangled it and strung it from one tree to another and then, with an elegant bow that reminded me of his juggling performance, he offered it to me. I laid myself in the hammock and asked, "How did you learn English, anyway?"

He shrugged. "A guy. *Un maestro.*"

I waited for him to add more, but he didn't. He pushed gently on the hammock, and I swayed under the restless trees.

"Did he teach you juggling and stuff, too?"

He nodded.

"Did you see me that day I took a nap in this?" I asked.

He didn't have to speak to answer that. He nodded slowly, and the hammock went on swinging under his gentle touch.

"What about the accident? The steering wheel?"

He looked away from me and kept his fingers knotted in the hammock string, allowing them to go back and forth, to slow me down, to stop the movement entirely. This time, he took my hand as I longed for him to do, and he used his finger to make the number 2. "Long," he whispered, and my ride in the swing was over.

Thirty-nine

We hadn't kissed except for the one time with the loquats. But on August 21, three days before the return to school, clouds rippled overhead like dirty fleece, turning the river into a room lit evenly from within.

I had the whole day off, so I had ridden into the canyon early, passing one woman on horseback and another with an off-leash Labrador. I hated the off-leash dogs. They found their way to Amiel's house fairly often and carried ramen bags away in their mouths.

I knew that what we were going to do that day was catch *cangrejos*. It turns out that *cangrejos del mar* are crabs, but *cangrejos del río* are crayfish, and that was the kind Amiel meant when he said they were his favorite food. Amiel allowed me to bring things now and then to contribute to our picnics at the river—a nice frying pan, a batch of brownies, matches—but this time he'd asked me to bring liver as bait for the *cangrejos*. Lamb liver. I handed it over, and he opened the grocery store package with his knife.

A crayfish trap, or at least a crayfish trap made by Amiel, looks like a collapsible wire basket. The lamb's liver goes in the bottom, and the long chain that comes up from the center is tied to an old plastic milk jug. Amiel had three of these traps, and once he'd baited them all and attached the floats, he led me to a place along his side of the river where little holes in the sand meant crayfish. Amiel dropped the baskets carefully in the water and led me further up the bank to sit. I had secretly brought something besides lamb's liver to share: the French mime movie that I'd watched back in May and tried to show him before he tapped my laptop shut.

"Come on," I said. "Do we have to watch the traps the whole time?"

He shook his head, but he seemed to think watching them would be ideal.

"Come *on*," I repeated. I made him follow me into his house—not the roofless old cottage where we cooked, but the grotto. I knew we could see the screen better there because the clouds made it even darker than usual, and I settled on the floor with my back to the wall. I patted the ground. He hesitated. Finally, he sat beside me, but I could tell he was thinking about his crayfish traps. "Just watch the beginning," I said.

Les Enfants du Paradis began, and I shifted the laptop a little so that he could see it better—one half of the keyboard on his leg, one half on mine. I thought he liked it, but I wasn't sure. He might have nodded now and then to make me *think* he liked it.

At the intermission, I said, "Do you like it?"

Another nod. *"Los cangrejos,"* he said, and went to check the floating milk jugs, so I followed him. When Amiel lifted them to show me, he grinned at the crayfish that were stuck there, six of them sucking down the lamb's liver.

We boiled them over the fire in the roofless house. Pretty soon I had to follow Amiel's example as he poked a fork inside the red shells of the crusty things and plucked out bits of crabby stuff. He began to extract whole lumps of chubby meat, while I just kept shredding it, and when he saw my clumsy efforts, he held out his fork of cray meat for me to take with my mouth. At first he was laughing, but as the meat got closer to my mouth, he stopped. I took the bite and chewed. He wiped my lower lip with his finger and then he leaned back. After that, he ate his crayfish and I ate mine. The weather had turned hotter, and I was desperate for a swim, a thing, strangely, we'd never done together. I wasn't wearing a swimsuit, but it was so hot and humid that I wanted to duck under the water in my clothes.

"I'm going to swim," I said. Sometimes, if I knew the Spanish word for something, I liked to show off. *"Nadar,"* I said. *"Yo."*

He gave me the look my Espanish deserved, but I walked to the deepest spot on his side of the river, dramatically plugged my nose, and plunged in. I have to admit I wondered if the crayfish would mistake me for lamb's liver. I treaded water and then, gingerly, let my feet touch bottom. "Amiel?" I said.

He appeared on the bank and stepped out of his shoes.

He took off his shirt.

Unmoored, I looked away. That was all he removed, though. He stepped into the water as you would step off a cliff, still wearing his jeans, and the two of us laughed. The skies got darker and heavier until the thing that almost never happens in summer here happened: it began to sprinkle and, briefly, to rain. It didn't last, but for a while we swam in the dimpled water and listened to the drops falling on all the sun-warmed rocks and roasted dust.

It stopped within fifteen minutes, and we climbed onto a table rock to dry. The air smelled sharply of minerals and lead. I saw the hats of walkers on the other side of the river, heard their voices and the jingling collar of a dog. I ducked my head, though we were doing nothing wrong. I thought briefly of my computer in Amiel's house, but I didn't want to go back there and check on it. If I did, it would seem like I was collecting my things, and if I collected my things, the day would end. I would have to go home.

Instead, I gestured for Amiel to follow me to the roofless house where we'd cooked the crayfish and drowned the fire. I didn't have a plan. I was vaguely sleepy, vaguely hungry. The ruin had a strange glow in the aftermath of the rain, the old white stucco bright against the spent gray clouds. The sharp mineral scent of the air gave way to woodsmoke and fish scales as we stood in the center of the wide-open house, and the silence became something you could feel all over, like cold. I didn't know what to do, so I stuffed my hands into my pockets, which were still wet, so I couldn't get more than my fingertips in.

"Why won't you tell me about the accident?" I asked.

Amiel stood near me, and I felt the old helplessness, when what I wanted to say I couldn't say. He reached down for his whittled stick and said hoarsely that after his father stopped sending money, his grandfather decided Amiel's mother should be his wife. "Mi *abuelo*," he said, either translating the word for "grandfather" or emphasizing the outrageousness of it.

"One day I saw him to hurting her," he said, and he coughed, paused, started again. "I said I was going to tell my *tío*."

I knew *tío* meant "uncle," so I waited. Amiel balanced the stick upright on his palm. He bounced it once, caught it, and bounced it again.

Looking at the stick, not me, he said hoarsely, "Mi *abuelo* let go of my mother to come after me with a rope." Amiel found a piece of string on the ground and tied it tightly around the stick. "*Así*," he said. Then Amiel let the stick fall, jerked on the string, and pulled the stick around in the dirt.

I just stared at him for a few seconds. "So there wasn't a car accident or a steering wheel?"

"No," Amiel said. He untied the string, wadded it up with his fingers, and let it fall. He drew a circle in the dirt with the stick, then took my hand and pulled me gently until I stood in the center of it. He drew my arm straight out and turned my palm upward. Then he stepped into the circle behind me until

207

his bare chest was pressed lightly against my back. While my hand trembled, Amiel tried to balance the stick upright on my palm. It stayed upright for only a second and then fell outward, and I was unwilling to step away from him to catch it.

Still pressed against my back, Amiel drew my arm back toward us and with his index finger began to trace letters on my forearm, his fingers as cold as rain. I felt the letters he was making on my skin, felt them all the way to the backs of my knees, but I was powerless to read them. The lines might have been hieroglyphics or flying birds. My arm trembled with each stroke until he reached the end of what he was writing and held still, my arm still propped in his arm, his breath near my left ear, his upper body bare. I waited, and he waited, and then he started again. I don't know if it was a new word or the same word, but I saw clearly this time that he was spelling, as I once had, *PLEASE*.

This time when we kissed, he didn't pull away, and I was close enough to his mouth for him to whisper what the tiny old vaquero had said a long time ago, the part about being of two worlds.

Tú eres de dos mundos.

I closed both of my eyes, the blue one and the brown one, so I could be in just one world, his, and as he kissed me, I understood what the silkworms were conjuring when they swayed and spun a coffin egg so tight and hollow they could disappear into its filaments. I touched with my finger the black disk on the hollow of his neck, he kissed my mouth and my neck and my eyes, and for the time that he held me there in the circle he'd drawn, what I wanted and what I had were the same.

A motorized roaring, loud and furious, finally made us pull away. Helicopters fly over Fallbrook all the time, usually marines training at Camp Pendleton, but sometimes they're the small white police helicopters looking for criminals who are being chased on the ground.

I opened my eyes to look up, and I saw the white body of a police helicopter zipping north in the air above us. It wasn't low enough for me to think the pilot was looking right at us, but it was low enough for me to feel exposed in the roofless house. I still didn't want to let go of him, but Amiel broke free and began scrambling into the hollow where the tree roots led to the river.

I followed him, and I heard the helicopter move above us to the south. We crashed our way through the willow shrubs and ducked into his safe little house, as dark as a rabbit's burrow, silent and cool until you heard, coming closer again, the ominous thwapping overhead.

"Have they done that before?"

"Sí," Amiel said. He pulled a dry shirt from a bag and put it on.

I wanted to resume kissing, and I tried, but he held himself like a person turned to stone. His gold-flecked eyes were dark as mud.

"They can't see us now," I said.

Amiel shook his head. He picked up my computer and slipped it into my backpack.

"Okay," I said coldly. "You want me to go."

He nodded very slowly.

"But I don't get it. They're not looking for you. They can't be."

He shrugged. He looked deliberately away from me. I remembered, although I didn't want to, what Hickey had said about prostitutes working in the reeds over in Carlsbad, and the arrest of Hoyt's worker at the grocery store, and the border patrol checkpoint on the interstate two miles east of where we sat, where the officers stood in the road at randomly chosen times and stopped traffic in all four lanes, looking without expression into each car before deciding who could go forward and whose car would be searched by dogs.

"But if I leave now, won't they notice me?" I pictured the aerial view of the river and how my head, like a moving figure in a video game, might call attention to the roof of Amiel's house.

Amiel listened tensely for the helicopter, and I pictured the border patrol agents waiting in their cars along the highway in Rainbow, parked cars I saw so often that I barely noticed them. Now I wondered what would stop them from coming here.

Amiel pulled me to the wall, and he sat down. I sat down with him. He kept his knees close to his chest, and I sat in the same position, too scared to move. We waited like that until we heard nothing but the slosh of the river against the banks and the mourning doves in the trees. *You knew*, they always seemed to be sighing in their disappointment. *You knew who knew.*

I looked at Amiel's face and felt the pull of him.

He kissed me once, soberly, and then he stood up so that I knew I had to go. His eyes had deepened now to shadows, but the trees outside his door floated in amber. The clouds had parted enough to let the setting sun gild the water. I crossed the river and turned to wave, but I saw nothing except willows and the orange spots that burned into my mismatched eyes.

Forty

School started. It was unremarkable except that Robby and I could now drive unchaperoned to school. He took us in his birthday car on the first day.

Me: How was Paris?

Robby: Oh, you know. Totally superior in all ways to the home sod.

Me: Really?

Him: No. I like the museums, though, and walking by the Seine.

He said *Seine* perfectly.

Me: How was Monsieur Pouf?

Him: Who?

Me: The ancient *le* tortoise. Your mother was telling me.

Him: He mostly hangs out in the garden. I was back there

one time, just kind of giving my parents some space, and there he was, smoking the last Gauloise.

Me: The last what?

Him: It's a French cigarette. They don't make them anymore. Monsieur Pouf, though, he has his sources.

Me: So what's the deal with the whole . . . you know, your dad and Mary Beth.

Him: I think I've persuaded her to switch.

Me: I know. She came to see me at Subway. To ask me why you dropped her.

Him: What did you say?

Me: I said I didn't know.

Him: Good.

Me (feeling kind of mean): So how do you know, anyway?

Him: Know what?

Me: That she's given him up?

Significant pause.

Him: I just do.

Me: But you didn't *specifically* talk about it.

Him: No. Of course not.

Me (trying to make him feel guilty): She seemed really nice.

To this he had no reply. We were almost to the school and I could see the ag buildings in the wet morning light.

Him: What about you, though?

Me: Me?

Him: Have you been—*hunh hunh hunh* (Robby's impression of Pepe Le Pew)—*fabricating zee love* while I was gone?

Me (*turning a suspicious crimson color*): Why would you think that?

Him: Lucky guess. What's all that stuff in the tree house, by the way?

Me: The shells? Just stuff I found.

Luckily, we could hear the late bell through the windshield as he darted into a parking space, and we both had to make a dash for it.

Forty-one

My mother and Hoyt grew up in Idaho, and she says Fallbrook has two seasons: Green Grass, which lasts from January to April, and Fire Alert, which lasts the rest of the year.

For me, though, Fire Alert didn't start until October. Summer was supposed to be hot, and if September was hot, well, that was normal, too, because in northern places, which I'd read about in novels, that's when you had Indian summer.

But that September was a lilac bush roasting in the sun. Every day, the leaves baked until they were dry, brittle, and pale. The ground turned to rock. And then, all of a sudden, there was a hot wind, like when you lean over a fire pit where you've piled newspaper and cardboard and some kindling and you blow all the breath you have in order to make it bloom into flame.

On September 13, we were the kindling, and a monstrous

god leaned over us to breathe. Clouds melted, brush trembled, and the ocean burned white like molten glass. Palm fronds crashed into roads. Leaves swirled in the parking lot. My nose bled and my skin cracked. I breathed cotton-dry breaths through paper lips and dreamed of Amiel in the heat.

By the middle of the night, the wind was like a dry hurricane. It was furious with the house, furious with the trees, enraged by every last one of us. It threw things at the windows and it beat on the roof. I was reading *For Whom the Bell Tolls* and my mother was dreaming her sleeping pill dreams, and at 2 a.m., exhausted, I put the book down and covered my head with the blanket and repeated my mantra, *Go to sleep go to sleep go to sleep*.

I was hoping, like everyone else who lay awake listening to the wind, that no pyromaniacs were out there, trembling in thrall beneath the god monster, reaching for a match.

Go to sleep go to sleep go to sleep gotosleep.

I said it, but I didn't listen. Then finally, around three o'clock, I guess I did.

Forty-two

Fires started twice when my father was still at home, always in October, always to the west of us, where most of the hills were used for training by the marines. Both times, my father kept saying casually, "It's farther than it looks." He said it the year forty-seven houses burned in Fallbrook, and he was right. Those houses were three miles from us, not three hundred feet, as it appeared in the dark.

From our former house, which was on a hill, we could watch fires as they licked their way up hillsides in the dark, and we could follow the tiny red lights of planes dropping scoops of water, and we could hear the sirens as the fire engines screamed west on Mission Road, and we barely slept on those nights, getting up every half hour to go to the windows and see if the fire had moved any closer.

Just before dawn on September 14, I heard my mother's

cell phone ring. It was the school dispatcher giving her a job subbing at Mary Fay Pendleton, the elementary school out on the marine base. It was second grade, which she liked, because at that age kids still wanted to hug you, even if you were just there for one day, and the worst thing that ever happened was a kid shouting, "My tooth fell out!"

"I smell smoke," I said.

"The power's out," my mom said, flipping the light switch to no effect.

I looked at the empty face of the digital clock and turned the button on the radio. Nothing.

We went outside in our pajamas. Lavar's house was low inside the grove, and you couldn't see anything but avocado trees. The god monster was still blowing hard on all of us, and the branches shook.

"Where do you think it is?" I asked, turning around and around. It was already warm outside, like an oven you've just turned on.

We looked at the sky again, and I spotted the plume.

"It's always farther than it looks," my mother said, shielding her eyes, and then she turned to walk indoors.

I wondered if she knew she sounded like my father. "Don't you think we should stay home?" I asked. I wanted to go to the river and find Amiel.

"Oh, it's probably thirty miles away and ninety percent contained," she said, letting the screen door flap shut. "Hurry or we're going to be late."

I was still dubious, but my uncle Hoyt called my mother to

say he'd checked with the high school and they had electricity. I could hear his voice from clear across the room. "School's in session, they told me," he said. "Robby's going."

"Is Robby going to drive?" I asked her to ask him. I wanted to ride with Robby instead.

"He'll drive if he can find his car keys," came the voice.

"Robby can ride with us," my mother told him. "We're leaving in fifteen minutes. Do you know where the fire is?"

"East," the phone voice seemed to shout. "I'm going to hop on my bike and check it out. I'll let you know later on, okay? Keep you updated." When Hoyt said "bike," he meant his off-road motorcycle, so my mother said okay.

My only option was to pretend it was a normal day, except that you couldn't run a hair dryer, coffeemaker, microwave, or toaster. You couldn't see yourself in the bathroom mirror because the bathroom was so dark. My mother stood by the living room window and looked in the mirror over the fireplace to put her hair up in a bun. I did a ponytail the same way. She took an Excedrin to replace her cup of coffee. Robby, frazzled and furious from not finding the car keys, met us at the Oyster.

"I even looked in the pool," he said.

It wasn't until we reached the overpass that I had a good look at the eastern sky. West of us, above Fallbrook and the river, the sky was blue, but behind us, it was Armageddon brown.

"I think we should turn back," I said. "We should pack our stuff."

"I can't be late," my mother said.

219

Robby twisted his head around to scrutinize the cloud. "Relax," he said. "My dad'll check it out. He'll get pretty close and let us know if there's any danger."

"Right," my mother said, accelerating.

She kissed me goodbye on the cheek in the high school parking lot. She didn't normally do that anymore, and it made me nervous. The air still had that campfire smell, but from the parking lot, the huge milky stain in the sky was invisible. Some hills and houses were blocking it.

"Whatcha le think?" I asked Robby. I stood looking in the direction of the hidden smoke.

"About the fire?" he asked. He shrugged. "I think air quality's gonna be low, so they'll cancel PE today."

I thought of this as a positive, but Robby looked glum.

"See you at lunch?" I asked.

"Right," he said. "Meet you by the flagpole."

But we didn't make it to lunch. At the end of second period, Mr. K. came on the loudspeaker and announced that school was canceled. Buses would run. Parents had been notified. Evacuation orders had been issued to parts of Fallbrook, Rainbow, and Pala, so we should proceed home.

Kids in my history class pulled out their cell phones and turned them on. I did the same, and as we all lifted our heavy backpacks, the doors of every classroom clanked open and out flowed a river of students with phones clapped to their ears. Soon the quad was a sea of backpacks and people staring nervously into space as they had conversations with people who weren't there.

My mother had already left me a message. She said she had to stay in her classroom until every single child was signed out. "Go home with Robby and Uncle Hoyt," she said. "Stay with them, and I'll meet up with you when I can leave here."

Robby was standing at the flagpole, his backpack slumped casually by his feet. "Weren't you just totally Cassandra this morning?" he said.

"Who's that again?" Robby disliked all fiction except Tintin and Greek mythology, so I assumed Cassandra was Greek.

"She foretold the future, but she was also cursed so that everybody always doubted her."

"Yes, then. Cassandra, *c'est moi*."

"My dad said my mom's freaking out and packing stuff. We got a reverse 9-1-1 call."

I'd never heard of this.

"They dial *in* instead of *out*," he said. "Instead of you calling the emergency people, they call you."

"Oh," I said. "Did your dad go see the fire?"

"He said he tried. It's not that far away. He said he's filling the truck up with gas and we've got to find a place to stay."

"Where are we supposed to go?" I asked.

"Not up 15," Robby said. "The freeway's closed."

It was as if he'd said the sky was closed. "Closed? Then how's everyone going to get out?"

"The other way," he said. "You have to get to the 5," which was the other eight-lane freeway going north or south but along the coast. Getting to the coast freeway could be difficult even on Sundays, when people in Fallbrook and Temecula and

Vista tried to go to the beach on a winding road that was just two lanes wide.

In other words, we were in a maze with two exits, and one of them was on fire.

Just then Greenie and Hickey found us. "Can you believe this?" she said. "How're you getting home?"

"My mom can't leave her school until all the little kids get picked up," I said. "So we're waiting for Robby's dad."

Hickey said, "Call him and tell him I'll take you. I've got my car."

Robby thought about it for a few seconds, and then he called his dad. He said the school parking lot was a mess so it'd be faster to go with Hickey.

"I'll meet you at Greenie's house, then," I heard Hoyt shouting through Robby's phone. "The line at the gas station is getting really—hey, it's my turn, all right? I'll see you there."

Forty-three

The Coombs house was chaotic. They hadn't received an evacuation order, but they were packing both cars, anyway. Boxes of baby pictures, file folders, suitcases, and a tub of dog food sat by the front door. Greenie's brother was packing his Star Wars action figures and Mr. Coombs was calling hotels in Las Vegas.

"You're going all the way to Las Vegas?" I said to Greenie. It was a four-hour drive.

Greenie said, "That's weird," and went upstairs to find her mother.

Robby, Hickey, and I sat uneasily on the couch. The huge TV was on, and we couldn't help watching the news, which was mostly aerial pictures of burning hills, the strange empty lanes of the closed interstate, the slow thick lines of cars moving south where the freeway was open. Clouds of smoke the size of continents rose above them. Sometimes the camera zoomed in to show fire licking at bushes and roaring out of trees, but when the newscaster talked about where the fire was moving, he identified towns and neighborhoods far away from Fallbrook. There was more than one fire burning at the same time, and the one we were watching was near San Diego.

"I don't get it," Robby said. "Is that the reason we're being evacuated? That fire's like thirty miles away."

We watched some more, and the screen went to a map that showed a series of red dots. Each dot had a name. Each dot was a different fire. The one by Fallbrook was called "Agua Prieta."

"There's our fire," Hickey said.

Agua Prieta was the creek where I'd eaten loquats with Amiel, and if the fire was burning there, he was right in its path. "All of Fallbrook is under mandatory evacuation orders," the newscaster said.

With a sick feeling I couldn't tell Robby or Greenie about, I went to the backyard so I could look into the canyon. The sky was a dull peach color, not blue, and the air in front of me was flecked with bits of ash. The trees in the canyon looked dry in the haze, not green but khaki, and the wind made them lean and rattle. Would Amiel know if a fire was coming? He had no television and no phone. I'd never even seen a radio.

From where I stood, I heard Greenie's voice. "If we're going to Las Vegas," she asked, "can Hickey come?"

"No," her mother said. "No! Of course not. He should go home right now. Isn't his family worried about him?"

"Of course they're worried about him. But he was making sure I'm okay. He brought me home first, if you didn't notice. And Robby and Pearl."

"I appreciate that," Greenie's mother said. "But he should go now. You can bring Pearl with you to Las Vegas if you want. She's welcome."

Greenie didn't answer, or if she did, she'd moved too far away from the window to be heard. I walked to the edge of the yard, where a dry lilac bush clung to a rocky slope. I snapped off a sprig and crushed it easily to dust. It would only take ten or fifteen minutes to hike down to Amiel's house and see if he was okay. Then we could walk back out together.

I heard a chugging engine, and when I turned, my uncle was pulling to a stop by the mailbox and opening his door. He started to adjust the straps that held his dirt bike upright in the truck bed, and for some reason—fear, maybe, or an awareness of how quickly I would have to act in order to hide the details of my plan from everyone—I ran toward him.

"Hi, Pearly," he said. "You okay?"

"Yeah, I'm fine. Just a little scared." I was shaking all over, so he hugged me.

"Well, let's go, all right?" he said. "Is Robby inside?"

"Yeah, but Hoyt?" I said. "The Coombs are going to Las Vegas."

"Do they have relatives there?" he asked.

"No," I said, pulling my hair out of my mouth. The wind was stronger at the front of the house where there were no trees to block it. "But they've invited me to go with them," I said. Which was true. I'd heard that.

"Did you call your mom?" Hoyt said.

"She didn't answer her phone yet. I'm going to keep trying." And I was going to keep trying. I was going to keep trying to tell her I was going to Las Vegas.

Just then the front door of the Coombs house opened. I expected it to be Mr. or Mrs. Coombs, and if my uncle said something about how I was going with them to Las Vegas, I would really have to go, and Amiel would burn to death in the canyon because he had no television, no radio, no phone, and no car.

But it wasn't Mr. or Mrs. Coombs. It was Robby. "Hey, Dad," he said.

The door closed behind him.

"Pearl's going to Las Vegas with Greenie," Hoyt told him. "We'd better get going before your mother calls me again."

"Where are we going?" Robby asked.

"To the Gaudets'," Hoyt said. "They have room for us and they're near the 5."

I didn't know who the Gaudets were, but it turned out they were a family from the Alliance Française of San Diego.

"Oh, great," Robby said. He walked over to the truck and slung his backpack into the truck bed. I wanted them to leave. I wanted them to hurry. If they stayed in front of the house for ten more seconds, I knew Mrs. Coombs would come out.

"Well, bye," I said, and I started walking backward.

"Keep your phone on," my uncle said, and I hugged them both, even Robby, which felt weird because Robby and I weren't huggers.

"I will," I said, but some part of me that wanted to be truthful said, "The battery's getting low, though. I forgot to plug my phone in last night, and we didn't have any power this morning."

Hoyt stopped walking to the driver's side of the truck. He stood still and looked into his phone.

"Here," I said, my whole body listening for the front door to open and the screen door to creak. "Give me your phone, Robby." I typed Greenie's number into Robby's phone, and then I turned around. "Greenie's waiting for me," I said, and I hoped Robby and Hoyt wouldn't think it strange that I went to the backyard instead of the front porch. I held my breath when I got out of sight, still shivering all over, and I held my hand to the rough stucco of Greenie's house until I heard the roar of the Packrat's engine. Then, taking just one more glance at the house, I ran to the lilac bush and began to pick my way down the rocky slope to the river.

Forty-four

When I reached the bottom, the sky was yellow-brown and my shoes held buckets of dirt. My teeth clacked together, but the air was hot and I felt like a turkey trapped alive in one of those super-smokers. I tried not to think about the family in Valley Center that had tried to evacuate in the last fire like this. Two sisters were in a car trying to outrun the flames, but the flames caught up. One girl died, and the other lived in a burn unit for most of the next year.

My phone made its first warning beep, and I ignored it. I knew I had to call my mother again, but I wanted to find Amiel.

The smoke was air and the air was smoke, like standing upwind of a bonfire you couldn't see. The reeds along the river were scissor gray, and water flowed through them with no particular hurry except where wind ruffled the surface. I could see the upper story of trees bending near Amiel's house, and I wanted to scream, "Amiel," but something told me to wait. I tore off my shoes and started sloshing.

Right away I could see something was wrong. Sometime in the last two days, sticks and twigs had been thrown everywhere, some of them the size of tree limbs. Amiel's tin pot lay beside a plastic bag. One of his T-shirts had been ripped and thrown into a tree. "Amiel?" I said. When I'd walked a few more yards, I could see that his carefully woven wall of branches had been torn apart, exposing his house. His frying pan, his blanket, his enameled tin box, and a smashed package of ramen noodles had been flung down and soaked with water. On the wall, someone had written in red paint, YOUR NEXT.

"Amiel?" I called. I checked the fork of the flapping sycamore tree where he'd hidden from me once, but the fork was empty.

I went to the thicket where he normally hid his bicycle, but it wasn't there, and again I heard my phone beep. This time, I looked at it and saw the message: low battery.

Sometimes, when my battery is low, the best thing to do is turn off the phone. I always have more power when I turn it back on later. I held the button down like I was smothering a small plastic animal.

"Amiel?" I called, feeling a new level of panic. I tried to think he could be at work. He could be doing his regular Tuesday job, which was gardening for a friend of Hoyt's, and that's why his bicycle wasn't there. If Amiel was at work, maybe he didn't know his house had been torn apart by people with poor grammar skills.

It didn't seem likely, though. If you get a reverse 9-1-1 call to evacuate your house, do you tell the gardener to keep trimming the hedge?

I stuffed my sandy feet into my shoes, leaving my wet socks in the wreckage of his house, and I forced my way through the willows to the other slope, the one that led up to the homestead where we cooked. "Amiel?" I called again.

I heard a strange foghorn call, a low hoot like a cowbird or a bird-cow. It was coming from inside the roofless house.

When I stumbled through the open door, I found Amiel sitting on the floor, holding his hands to his lips like a mini–conch shell.

"What happened?" I asked.

He put one finger to his lips. I expected his body to be warm, but when I crouched down and tried to hug him, his arms and chest were as chilled as my sockless feet. He was solid and tense and still. It felt very good to be out of the wind.

"Yesterday," he whispered. "While I am working."

"We have to get out of the river," I said. "The fire is really big. Really, really big."

He nodded. He didn't move.

"Where should we go?" I asked. I was feeling all prickly inside.

He didn't shake his head or nod or make a suggestion. He stayed down.

"No," I said. "I mean we *can't* stay here."

It could be that Amiel always had a radio, and I just didn't notice it before. He had a small handheld radio now, in any case, and he turned it on. Two men were speaking Spanish to each other and then to a caller, who was a woman, and she sounded pretty upset. There are certain words everyone knows if you live near the border. *La migra*, for example, means "border patrol."

"I don't think the border patrol would arrest people fleeing from a fire," I said.

He looked at me with conviction. "*Sí*," he whispered. "Listen."

I listened to the Spanish voices, but I couldn't get more than a few words.

"Three people!" he said, and held up three fingers. "*Se los tomaron.*" The words, or maybe the smoke, made him cough.

"They won't take you if you're with me."

Again, the expression that he knew so much more than I did. I stood up to look east, in the direction the fire had been burning when I left home hours before, and I couldn't see a plume. For all I knew, that meant we were *in* the plume. "We have to get out of here!" I shouted. "Don't you understand me?"

Amiel took my hand and led me to the water and set me down on the bank. Then he stepped in and slipped his body lower and lower until he was sitting on the bottom. With his legs out, he could lie back and be completely submerged. "*Así*," he said, when he raised his head above the water and breathed. "Like this."

He meant we could survive in this shallow part of the river if the fire came, and I remembered something. During the Fallbrook fire we had watched from our house when I was twelve, a group of people who didn't evacuate fast enough got surrounded, the road was blocked, and they all survived by huddling in a backyard pool.

"No," I said. "I can't. I'm too scared."

"Go," he told me, his voice raspier from all the smoke. "*Yo estoy bien.*"

An hour had passed since I'd left Greenie's backyard. I sat on the bank beside Amiel and dug my phone out of my pocket. I shivered. I still hadn't talked to my mother, so I turned it on. When the phone woke up enough to show me messages, I listened to my mother say, "*I talked to Hoyt and I'm hoping to get out of here soon. I wish you had asked me before you went with someone else. Kind of worries me to be separated. Anyway, I'm glad you're safe. Should we let your dad know, maybe? Call me.*"

The next message said, "*Call me.*"

And the next.

And the next.

Then she said, "I'm going to try Greenie's mom."

I was sitting there trying to think what to do when the phone began ringing in my hand. The screen said the person calling was my mother. I was conscious of Amiel lifting himself out of the river, of water running off his clothes, of muscles and skin that I wanted to touch the way that I wanted to breathe.

"Where are you going?" I asked, and he pointed toward his

house. I wanted to turn on the radio and hear someone say, in English, that the fire was one hundred percent contained.

Instead, my phone rang again. I stared at it the way you might stare at the inside of your front door when you know it's either the police or the psychopathic killer on the other side.

Either my mother knew by now that Greenie's mom had no idea where I was, or she hadn't been able to reach Greenie's mom and I could, by answering the phone, put off that discovery a little longer.

"Mom?" I said.

"Where *are* you, Pearl?" my mother said, and I knew I'd opened the door at the wrong time.

"I'm fine," I said automatically, as if that would help.

"Where are you being fine? I just talked to Greenie's mom."

"I had to check on someone," I said.

"You had to *check* on someone?"

My ability to lie was like my ability to speak Spanish. I didn't have the speed, the fluency, or the verb tenses. "I just, yeah, I had to."

"I'm driving to the coast," she said, enunciating all the words you would capitalize in the title of a story or play. "Hoyt and Agnès Are Driving to the Coast. We Are Driving to the Coast on Separate Roads and *We Are Meeting There*. Do you have any idea what's going on here, Pearl? Are you still in Fallbrook? Is that what you're not telling me?"

"Yeah, but I'm fine. I have a way out," I said. I was looking at the water and thinking about what it would be like to sit in the river while a fire burned over us. Wouldn't we die from inhaling smoke? How would we breathe?

"With whom?" my mother demanded.

I had no power to answer.

"With whom, Pearl?" my mom said. "Okay, I'm stopping the car. I'm going to have to turn around. If they'll let me. I'm still on Camp Pendleton, you know. They've opened the road to civilians to make another road out. Opened the road through the *base*, Pearl. Do you have any idea how serious this is? Oh my God. It's a boy, isn't it? You're with a boy. Just tell me how he's getting you out of there and I'll meet you at the pier in Oceanside. I don't care who it is. Just stop lying to me."

I turned around and watched Amiel's wet back. *Wetback*, I thought. The ugly name for immigrants who swam across the Rio Grande. Just then my phone beeped to tell me my time was running out.

"Um, my battery's going dead," I said.

It was good, in many ways, that my phone was dying. A near-dead phone keeps you from knowing, for a while, that your father, during the largest evacuation in state history, doesn't call to see how you are. Not once. Nada. No thought whatsoever for your safety. A near-dead phone keeps you from talking to the best friend you've used as an alibi. It keeps you from stumbling through another set of half lies to explain to your mother why you're walking to a ruined house with a boy who's more afraid of police than of wildfires.

"I'm pulling over," my mother said. "I'm going to find a

234

policeman or a marine or something, and we'll get to you. Tell me where you are."

"I'll call you with another phone as soon as I can," I said. "I promise."

I had to close the phone. I had to turn it off. Or I had to say, "I'm at the river with that boy we saw at the day-labor site, the one who works for Uncle Hoyt." I wanted to admit that to her, but there are things you think you can say, things you say in your mind, that never pass your lips. "I really will call you," I told her instead, and I closed the phone. Then, just before I followed Amiel to the house that gave no shelter, I pushed the button to Off.

Forty-five

When I was little, my mother used to do crafts with me. We'd press flowers and make waxed paper cards, or we'd sew pincushions out of felt and stuff them with sawdust from the neighbor's garage. But my favorite thing was this paper that made really primitive photographs called "sun prints." You set a piece of lace or a leaf or a skeleton key on the paper and let the sun shine on it for a few minutes, and then you dipped the paper in water. The paper turned blue, but the shadow of the object turned white.

When Amiel and I got back to the house, I turned the radio to a station where the news was in English. I sat down in front of it as if the foundation of the house were a giant piece of photographic paper. Amiel went away and changed his clothes and came back, dry except for his hair. It was two o'clock, and the sun was purple. I felt sick from breathing the smoke and sick from fear. I lay down, finally, on the blanket Amiel had placed beside the wall. I said, "We could go up to a neighborhood and find a car."

This made no sense. What car? I was going to steal a car? "We could get a ride with someone," I clarified.

All I'd have to do was explain to someone that my name was Pearl and I was separated from my mother because she was a substitute teacher who was out on the base today and my cell phone was dead.

Anyone would help me. Anyone at all.

And this is my friend, Amiel.

They would help him, too. They'd think he was a student at Fallbrook High. They wouldn't ask questions. Not during a fire.

I went through this in my mind until I was satisfied, and then I told Amiel how it would work.

He regarded me briefly, then said we shouldn't climb now. "*El fuego,*" he said, his voice worse and worse, choked as if he had laryngitis, "*se suben rápido.*" Fire. Rapid. I got that part. He used his hand to show something in flight, something zooming upward. The fire drills and assemblies of my childhood had taught me this, *hot air rises,* but I didn't know that it burns fast going uphill and slow coming down.

I tried, weakly, to say that we could go east, where it would be flat for a long time. He picked up the radio and turned the dial until he found an American station. "Well, at this point," a man was saying, "all four fires in San Diego County are zero percent contained. Rainbow, Fallbrook, Escondido, Rancho

Bernardo, Ramona, and parts of Julian are under evacuation orders. Winds are very high. If you haven't gotten out of those places, you need to get out now."

"Oh my God," I said.

Amiel sat very still and calm, watching the sky to the east. I lay down with my fists covering my eyes, my face toward the wall, knees locked in despair. In a sun print, I would have been the skeleton key.

I lay there thinking and trying not to think, trusting him to know when we should get in the water and fearing that no one could know when to get in the water. I felt his shadow and heard the scrape of his feet. He lay down beside me and put one arm over my waist, and we lay there front to back until I took the fists away from my eyes and turned around.

If you move something in a sun print, the edges blur. I felt the edges of myself blur into nothingness as I kissed Amiel and he kissed me, and I found in the abandon of kissing him, clothes on, bodies moving, a physical way to go where my mind had already gone: deep down into water that would let the fire pass over us. I sank deeper and deeper, swimming without effort or resistance, and he swam deeper, too, until we became the same swimmer, the same water, and were drowned.

All the time the radio voices were talking, but they weren't talking about any places we knew, and I began to shiver afterward and to hear them clearly again, and the voice said, "We go now to a press conference with the chief of the North County Fire District, and he's going to bring us up to date on the Agua Prieta Fire up by Rainbow and eastern Fallbrook."

I sat up, and Amiel did the same. We didn't look at each other as we listened. The sun was far enough in the west that it had taken on a weird, coppery glow. The fire chief said they were hoping for a change in the wind and that firefighters were on their way from Northern California and Oregon, but the fire had jumped I-15 at Rainbow and was burning through residential areas along East Mission Road, which meant Willow Glen.

The fire was coming toward us, and the wind was coming toward us, and I knew I couldn't spend a whole night waiting for the moment when we should submerge ourselves in a place where the river was just twelve feet across and two or three feet deep.

"There's deeper water," I said, remembering the spot on the river where Hickey and Greenie took me the day we ate lunch together. "Farther west of here. On the other side of the road. It's wider there, too, like a big pool."

Amiel looked at me like I made no sense, so I said, "I mean the De Luz Road. That way." I pointed west, away from the fire.

Amiel shook his head and pointed out the doorless door at the nearest bank of the river.

"Have you been that way? To the end of the trail?"

He shook his head again and kissed my neck. I wondered if there was a name for what we'd just done together. It wasn't sex, exactly. It wasn't necking, certainly, and it wasn't petting.

I wondered if it was normal to worry about sex things while you were also worrying about burning alive.

"We can walk along the water and not go uphill," I said in a shaky voice. "We can stay right near water the whole time so that if it catches up . . ."

But it was September, when the water was so shallow in places that you could never get all of yourself under it. I was unable to conjure a single part of the river that was fireproof. No matter where I went along the trail or the road from De Luz, black trees stuck out of the ground. Still, it had to be safer to move farther west, away from the fire they were talking about and into a place where the trees on either bank weren't so close together.

I reached out for Amiel's hand and he laced his hand into it. "Please," I said. "Please let's go to the deeper water."

He let his eyes look into mine with full force, as if my head were a room in which he would find something he'd lost. "*Si quieres*," he managed to say.

Not "yes." Not "okay," but "if you want."

Forty-six

My mom used to tell me every time we went camping or hiking or even to the park on a crowded summer evening, "If you get lost, hug a tree," the idea being that she could only find me if I stayed in one place.

I think now we should have followed Amiel's plan. If we had, we would have stayed in the place where Robby told my uncle to look, and he would have found us.

The timeline, as I have pieced it together, goes like this.

My mother pulls over, as she threatened, and gets out of her car. People in other cars stare at her. They ask if she's out of gas. She shakes her head. Most of the people have dogs in their cars. In a minivan, she sees a pair of llamas. They gaze at her with their long-lashed eyes, necks slightly bent. Trailers full of horses inch by, cats stare out of rear windows, fish float in aquariums, and birds fly in birdcages. Some people are holding goats. The whole exodus through Camp Pendleton is like a car-trip Noah's Ark, and my mother, standing to watch it, dialing my uncle, draws the attention of an armed marine in uniform, who drives along the shoulder from some sort of a checkpoint to ask her what she needs.

"My daughter's still in Fallbrook," she says. "I thought she was with my brother, but she isn't. I have to go back."

The marine says she can't go back. "How old is she?" the marine asks.

"Fifteen," my mother says.

The marine thinks it's one of those misunderstandings, a natural mistake, an innocent girl left alone in her house! *Poor thing!* he's thinking.

"Where's your house, ma'am?" the marine asks. He's all ready with his walkie-talkie.

"She's not there," my mother has to admit. Then she has to confess she doesn't know *where* I am and worse, that I won't tell her.

What kind of girl acts like this during the Largest Evacuation in State History?

"Do you want me to call the sheriff?" the marine offers. He's clearly stumped. "Hey, don't cry, we'll figure something out" comes along pretty soon after this. I know what this marine looks like, silver-haired and blue-eyed, and I know his name is Mitchell and that he's forty-eight and divorced because he called my mother a few days later to ask if she found me okay, which led to her telling him the whole story, which led to him saying would you ever want to have dinner

242

with me, and her saying that would be nice, and the two of them going to the same Ruby's on the pier where I went for my birthday a million years ago when I learned that scallops are sometimes the flesh of bat rays shaped with cookie cutters.

But for now my mother is still having a breakdown on the dirt shoulder of a marine base road. She's placing the missing persons report. And she's saying she'd like to make one more call, which the marine says is okay, and then he'll help get her back into the flow of traffic and out of harm's way.

She calls Hoyt.

Hoyt is just reaching the Gaudets' beach house. It's on a cliff in Solana Beach. A post-modern castle the color of burnt cream. My uncle has his motorbike lashed upright in the back of his truck and he's already planning how to sneak back through the roadblocks and check on his ranch, see if there's anything he can do to save it himself. He doesn't know it's already burning. The fire reports aren't that specific yet.

"Don't worry, Sharon," Hoyt tells my mother. "I'll call Marco, okay? My friend that works for Verizon. He can trace her phone, I'll bet, and figure out where she was when she called you."

Robby is standing there on the cliff in Solana Beach. He's been carrying boxes of his mother's things into the Gaudets' marble entryway. He's been toting suitcases and file folders and shoes.

"Who?" Robby stops to ask his father. It's still early in the afternoon. "Where *who* was when she called?"

"Hey, do you know where Pearl is?" my uncle asks Robby.

Hoyt tells my mother to hang on a sec because Robby might know.

Robby takes the phone from my uncle and my mother says right away, "Robby, does Pearl have a boyfriend?"

Robby can't think of one. "No," he says. "I thought she was kind of interested in that guy my dad hired, but I don't think it went anywhere."

My aunt Agnès is still moving in and out of the marble entryway of the Gaudets' stone house. She can see the worried looks, hear part but not all of the questions. Hoyt explains that I'm still in Fallbrook where I ought not to be and that I won't say who with.

In French or in English, Agnès comes to the right conclusion. Aunt Agnès knows the parakeet can't live with the tortoise, but it will certainly try. *Cherchez la femme*, I guess she thinks, though in this case it would be *Cherchez le hombre*. Agnès says it could be that worker, Amiel, and this dredges up Robby's memory of the jar of shells in the tree house and the day I made Robby promise he wouldn't tell anyone about the squatter's house.

Within the hour, my uncle is on his motorbike. He's wearing a helmet, leather jacket, and gloves. He's speeding in the wrong direction, against all the traffic streaming away from the fire, through air turned orange with ash.

Forty-seven

You know what California looks like when it's burning. Oakland, Santa Barbara, Malibu, Ramona, Escondido, Esperanza—from the air they all look the same: a white-hot fluttering edge of flame, smoke the color of chocolate milk, and, when night falls, the blackness that the bright edge of flame is devouring, foot by foot, mile by mile, bush by bush. You can't look away as it burns. You can't help but feel yourself in thrall.

I could hear planes overhead as we hurried west. Now and then we looked up to see helicopters. They were usually going the opposite direction—toward Willow Glen, Rainbow, and the Lemon Drop Ranch. I was always listening for what I imagined to be the sound of a traveling fire: a crackling hiss like what I heard in the fireplace but with the volume turned way up. I was always turning my head to see if the heat I felt on my back was a wall of fire, but when I looked back, I saw the same lifeless colors behind us: ink blue and ink brown. No candles of flame, no inferno, no reason to throw myself in the water we kept sloshing through or skirting around, more often than not no deeper than water running down your driveway when you wash the car.

We reached the plateau as the sun went out, a wide beach where the river could flood when we had heavy rain, though I had never seen it flood. Behind us, the woods fell into cindery darkness. I followed Amiel up a slope near the parking lot where I had once, last spring, climbed out of Hickey's car. I could just barely make out the De Luz bridge lying four feet above a concrete watershed. Curiously, it had no guardrail and no sides. Only a troll would be able to fit under it without crouching.

But just as we were about to walk out of the trees into the open, Amiel threw out his arm to stop me. A fire engine was wailing its long wail.

"*Esperete,*" he whispered. *Wait.*

The siren was deafening as it passed, and not far behind came an echoing wail.

"Why?" I whispered back, so hungry and terrified that I was half ready to jump in the path of the fire engine. "They would save us," I said, but he wasn't listening to me or he couldn't hear me over the noise. He was five feet away, running back into the plateau. The fire engine passed. Then another. And another. I didn't raise my hand or step out of the trees. I did what I thought was to love him, and I followed Amiel back down the bank toward the sheltering reeds.

Forty-eight

Smoke blotted out the stars. We didn't have Amiel's blanket
or food or anything, thanks to my plan, so we just sat down in
the sand and rocks, far from trees that could catch on fire. I
kept listening for the return of the fire engines, and I pictured
them stringing out across the riverbed to make a controlled
burn that would go east as the other fire came west, thereby
putting us right in the path of a whole new fire, but I figured
that would be pretty loud and we'd have time for me to run out
screaming with my hands up.

The engines didn't return, and the darkness into which I
stared so hard never roared into flame, and soon I stopped
hearing, stopped seeing, stopped knowing, asleep as I was
against Amiel, who lay like a cowboy in a John Wayne movie
with his head on his balled-up jacket. I used him as a pillow

and a sort of bed, one leg flung over his. Burrowing and gnawing into my sleep was the memory that I had never called my mother, and that memory chewed sleep to bits until I was awake again thinking, *What have I done?*

They say that parts of a teenager's brain aren't formed yet. That might have been the problem. I'd like to think that rather than a malignancy of heart.

I'm fine, I tried via ESP. *I'm fine I'm fineimfineimfine.*

I reached into my pocket and felt my phone as if it were a five-dollar bill I'd stashed in my pocket and forgotten. Amiel stirred, and he looked at me.

"I should call my mother," I said.

He nodded. I wanted to kiss him. I wanted us to be a married couple in deepest Mexico or a married couple in a fable about deepest Mexico.

Instead, I held the button down on my phone and learned that Greenie had sent words (WHERE R U?) and Robby had sent words (CALL MY DAD PLS) and my mother had called six hours ago.

"If you get this message, Pearl," my mother said, her voice taut, "call your uncle on his cell phone. He's going back on the motorcycle and he says he's going to look for you down at the river in some hut where Robby thinks you might have gone. Call him and tell him where you are, Pearl."

I did it. Right then. There could have been many reasons why he didn't answer.

He couldn't hear the ring over the motorcycle engine.

He couldn't hear the ring over the motorcycle engine.

He couldn't hear the ring over the motorcycle engine.

I spoke into whatever is listening when no one answers. I said, "It's me, Pearl." I was quiet for about ten seconds. Then I said I was by the De Luz bridge.

My impulse after saying these things was to erase the message, but I had reached a point where I didn't know a way to make things better and I feared making them worse. I didn't erase the message. I just hung up.

Amiel looked at me, and in my life that was not a fable, I told him that my uncle was looking for us at his house. "That way," I said, and pointed in the direction of the fire, which was also the direction of Amiel's house. "I'm afraid," I said, "that he won't leave" (punctuated by useless tears), "until he finds me. And he'll burn."

I wondered, as I tried to call my uncle again, what a phone that has burned in a fire would do with incoming calls. Did the fact that his phone didn't ring at all, that it went right to a recording of his voice saying, *Hello, hello, hello, please leave a message*, mean he was talking to someone else or listening to my last message? I hung up.

The water flowed fast and dark beyond the reeds. I looked down at my dirty shoes, pressed hard on my eyes, and wondered what would make this all come out right.

"*Ven,*" I heard Amiel whisper, "Come," and he stood up. "To find him."

He walked, sure-footed, ahead of me, and I stumbled

along, my hand in his. The rhythm of a story my mother used to tell me got stuck in my aching head:

Going on a bear hunt,

We're not afraid.

What a wonderful day!

Over and over, through the not-wonderful dark, scared and stumbling, between branches and trunks, *going on a bear hunt*. My hand stayed gripped in his hand, *we're not afraid*, and at last we thrashed our way through a stand of willows and *What a wonderful day* we were breathing hard and shivering at the edge of the grotto, so I called out, "Uncle Hoyt?"

We're not afraid.

I listened for a motorcycle engine and then remembered that on these narrow, rocky trails, in this smoky darkness, he would surely have to be on foot.

I pushed the button on my phone, but nothing happened. The battery had died while I was walking.

"Hoyt!" I shouted. Darkness, smoke, heat, and water swallowed the words.

Two things happened next that are still hard to believe, so dreamlike and monstrous did they seem. Amiel plunged into the water, and I, still connected by his hand, plunged in after him. The air was quivering with heat, and it smelled different. I became aware of a crackling sound and a rosy, hazy, blossoming glow. It was pink and orange and lathery. I was looking at the glow, which I knew was the fire, and I was sinking down into the water, which came only to my waist, when a light-colored shape streaked along the path where we'd been standing and was gone.

"*El léon,*" Amiel said, pulling me lower into the water.

I wanted to laugh and tell him there are no lions in California. What did he think? That we were in Africa? Then I remembered the stuffed mountain lion in the glass cage of the Museum of Natural History. The air was so hot that I couldn't think about the lion anymore, and I could see the flames now fingering the tops of trees.

What a wonderful day.

The fire cracked branches like bones, and then flames reached for another tree, and we sat in the cold water up to our necks, our legs straight out on the slimy river bottom, and then Amiel pushed my head under, which made me cough and strike out, but when I could see again, vaguely, he was ducking his own head under and I thought, with what little reason I still had, that he was dousing my head so it wouldn't be the next candle, and I felt so very sick, as if I were a hot air balloon that had to go on sucking up the heat of a fire burning directly beneath me. I swallowed the heated air because I had no choice, and my head went high into the darkness and became heavy and came back down. The fire went on cooking and eating the trees and we stayed where we were, hiding from it, hoping it would pass us by. I was fully conscious and I was delirious, freezing but not frozen, for hour upon hour upon hour. The fire never completely encircled us but burned along one side. We stayed where we were even after it burned past us, Amiel's arms tightly fastened around me. Toward the end of the long night, I began to imagine I had seen the long ghostly body of the mountain lion very clearly, that it had turned to regard us as it ran, and that it had cracked-marble, blue-brown eyes.

Forty-nine

I woke to a world that wasn't black but gray, and on the surface of the water below my chin floated soapy flakes of ash. Amiel felt me jerk awake and he released his hold on my waist. He stood up slowly, his clothes heavy with water and mud, and I did the same, an ache in my head so sickening that I shuddered. There was something heavy in my pocket: the drowned phone. In no direction could I see flames, though I suspected that the ashes on the burned side of the river would hold, like the ashes in a fireplace, pink burning coals. Even the water smelled like smoke.

A low droning sound became a loud droning sound, then a deafening thwap. The helicopter was low enough that I could see, briefly, a human being inside, and I imagined that the human could see us. The helicopter turned around and made another pass. Yes, someone was looking at us, but I couldn't think whether this was salvation or doom.

Most of the blackened trees were south of the river, but Amiel's side of the river was still green, so that was where we climbed out. I was shaking so hard I could barely walk. I hate to throw up, but I threw up. I kept walking so that I wouldn't be near the vomit and after a few steps found I couldn't walk anymore.

"I have to sit," I croaked to Amiel, wondering if this was how his throat felt most of the time. He turned and gestured to me to wait, and when he returned, he had a blanket for me. He'd brought a can of beans and a knife, which he used to punch a hole in the lid, but I couldn't swallow the beans he tried to feed me.

The droning sound returned, grew louder, hesitated, and went away. I shivered in the blanket, laid my head on Amiel's lap when he pulled me to him, and then was not conscious of anything beyond the long gliding mythical body of the mountain lion as it turned its head to see what I'd done until I heard voices and saw beside us the thick black boots and yellow tarp-like pants of a firefighter. Not one but three. The one with a cleft chin and a voice like cold water knelt down and started checking things a doctor would check.

"How'd you get down here?" he asked. He didn't sound angry, but I thought he would be angry soon.

"Have you found anyone else?" I asked, my voice not only hoarse but trembling. I kept expecting the air to heat up again and rush burning into my head. Amiel stood off to one side, coughing hard.

"What do you mean?" the firefighter asked. "Were there more of you?"

"My uncle came to look for us. On his motorcycle."

He didn't answer me, but he pressed his lips together and I saw the narrow-faced one exchange a look with him, then go off a little way to talk into his radio.

When two of them put me on a stretcher, I saw in Amiel's face the same look that the mountain lion had in my dreams, and I said they should put Amiel on a stretcher, too, but Amiel shook his head, and they thought he couldn't speak English.

"¿Hablas inglés?" the water-voiced man asked Amiel, but Amiel didn't respond.

"He saved me," I said. "We should call my mother," I finally thought to say. I was stuttering now. "And we should call my uncle."

The man with a narrow face who had talked into his radio asked for the phone numbers and I chattered them out through my teeth. In a few minutes I heard him say, "Mrs. DeWitt? This is Larry Greenworth of the fire department. I've got your daughter here and I just wanted you to know she's fine. Looks like shock and hypothermia, some smoke inhalation, but we're going to take care of that."

Pause. "The river bottom," he said. "Santa Margarita."

Pause again. "No," he said. "She mentioned that. We're going to look for him."

When that was done, he tried the number for my uncle.

"Not answering," he said. I heard in the distance the piercing, repetitive cry a squirrel makes when it senses danger.

"Let's go," one of the men said. A crow, black as the trees, floated over our heads.

They told Amiel to follow them because they had thick boots and they'd be able to make or find a path through any still-burning coals.

I was lifted up, and the trees wheeled above me like black snowflakes. It was not like riding in a canoe but a wheelbarrow race, where all four of my limbs were held by other people as they scrambled over uneven ground.

"What were you doing down here?" the foot carrier asked me. "Hiking?"

"Yes," I stuttered.

"Didn't you get the evacuation order?"

I closed my eyes. This question would lead to other questions, and then they would be so angry, so I closed my eyes and pretended to sleep until I really did fall asleep. I was asleep when we passed the charred rubber tires of a burned motorcycle. I was asleep when we passed under the burned canopy of Agua Prieta Creek, ghostly and hollow, where Amiel and I had once peeled loquats with our teeth. I was jolted awake by the voice of one of the firefighters saying, "What the—hey! Get back here!"

"Why's he running?" the one at my feet asked.

When I lifted my head, I saw Amiel running back toward the river.

"No," I tried to shout, my voice incapable of shouting.

"Should I go after him?" the firefighter who wasn't carrying me asked the others. He looked young and exhausted.

"No," the one holding my feet answered. He saw his chance to ask me questions again. "Who is he?"

I started to say Amiel's name and then stopped. "He worked here," I said. "He heard that the border patrol is waiting at the freeways t-t-t-to catch them."

We'd reached Willow Glen. A fire truck was there and an ambulance. To my surprise, the aloe field wasn't burned. The mailboxes stood in a row, mouths agape. The yellow cottage was still a yellow cottage. The black path of the fire lay to one side, through somebody else's house, which was now just a chimney and charcoal palms.

They slid me into the ambulance like I was the ginger-bread man, and I wanted to jump up and run away, but they popped an oxygen mask over my mouth. They wrapped my arm with a black Velcro cuff and held me down until it was clear that I had nothing to say in the matter, no power to run.

Fifty

One day after the fire, I dreamed Amiel was dead. He was face-down in the water, and the water was gray.

Fifty-one

Two days after the fire, I thought I saw Robby in the hospital room. "The ostrich died," he told me, his voice a hiss. "You killed it."

But when I asked my mother where Robby went, she said, "He was never here."

It still hurt to breathe and talk, and mostly I didn't want to talk, but a little while later I croaked, "Where's Hoyt?"

She didn't answer. The TV was off, and she had a newspaper on her lap.

"Is he mad at me?"

She didn't answer. The look on her face pressed me back like the force of an airplane gathering speed to take off. She'd been crying, but she wasn't crying now. She opened her mouth to say something she didn't say.

"He's okay, isn't he?" knowing he was not okay.

She shook her head and I knew that what she'd been cry-ing about was not me or the burned stuff in our house but whatever had happened to Hoyt.

"Did he get burned?" I said. "Is he in the hospital, too?"

More of the look that pressed me back. "He died, Pearl," she said. "He tried to outrun the fire on a slope."

Fifty-two

Three days after the fire, I woke up and Hoyt was still dead. I didn't hope Robby would visit; in fact, I feared now that he would.

Only my mother was willing to visit. "I want you to take a pregnancy test and an AIDS test," she said.

I shook my head.

"Are you *sure*," she said, her voice making it a statement instead of a question. "You know how you get it, right?"

I assumed she meant AIDS, and I nodded.

"You mean you didn't sleep with him or you used a condom?" she said. She wasn't good at this kind of conversation, or maybe I never seemed like the type to need it, and I could tell it pained her to ask.

I considered writing with my fingertip on my mother's thin

freckly arm: *Didn't have sex.* Instead, I used a Post-it note from my hospital tray table.

"Good," she said.

She didn't look like she believed me, and I couldn't blame her.

Fifty-three

Four days after the fire, while my mother was in the cafeteria, I turned on the TV in my room and learned that the fire wasn't over, that it wasn't contained, that it still flickered and burned. Power lines were down, and the National Guard still blocked Mission Road at the freeway, turning away people who tried to talk their way in.

The doctor said he couldn't keep me anymore, even though we'd lost our house, but he gave us the name of a hotel in downtown San Diego that was giving free rooms to people like us. I spent a number of hours there staring at windows that might or might not have been the windows of the condo my father had bought, in which he might or might not have been sitting at a desk that might or might not have been meant for me. I asked my mother if my father was in town.

"Who knows?" she said.

Then she took a call from a person who turned out to be Mitchell the marine.

Fifty-four

Five days after the fire began, most people were allowed to go back home, if they had homes. Louise Bart offered my mother the use of her RV, a little trailer covered in pine needles at the back of her farm on a road called Santa Margarita because it wasn't far from the river. The very first evening, I tried to go on foot to the trail, but my mother caught me.

"You know they're trying to determine if a squatter's camp started the fire, don't you?" she said.

"It wasn't his," I said.

"You're not going anywhere," she said, and she locked me in the trailer. A few minutes later, she came back and unlocked it. She called my name through the door and said, "I'm sitting right out here with Louise and her husband. You can join us for hamburgers when you want."

I didn't.

Fifty-five

Six days after the fire started, we stood in the ruins of the Lemon Drop Ranch. My mother crossed her arms and walked carefully over the rubbish. High above us, clouds webbed a turquoise sky. The fire had not burned everything evenly. The pine trees were uniformly black, like chandeliers dipped in tar, but the avocado trees were shriveled and brown, with leaves still rattling from limbs. You could see things from the cottage you couldn't see before, such as the crusty, tangled platter of Robby's house, where a hired crew was tearing out bits of junk and raking it into piles. Robby and his mother weren't there. They were at the Berry-Bell and Hall funeral home making arrangements.

Certain things were easy to identify in the crumpled piles of stuff: a mottled fork and a mottled spoon. Wires. A dusty but otherwise undamaged ceramic bowl. In the kitchen, near what used to be the stove, chrome had melted into silvery frosting. Photographs, letters, cabinets, books, sheets, towels, and napkins were unidentifiable dust. The silkworm ball was dust. The couch, the Yahtzee board, the librarian skirt. Quilts it took somebody a million hours to make. We didn't think of every lost possession right then, but over time, one by one, like a phantom limb.

"Remember when you burned your wedding pictures in the grill?" I asked my mother.

"Yes," she said.

"I guess you could have just waited."

She didn't speak, and I couldn't think why I'd said such a thing.

"I'm sorry," I said.

"I wouldn't have burned your baby pictures," she said, and she picked her way around a fallen clump of bathroom tile. It bothered and mystified us both that the iron sewing machine wasn't just sitting there intact. How could a sewing machine melt in a house fire? Why that and not a salad fork?

I dug around in the cold rubbish for a while and collected another fork, another spoon, and then I got up the courage to go closer to Robby's house. I was walking there when I realized I was stepping over the former site of the tree house, which was now a few metal braces and beams and piles of flaky charcoal. I found a stick and poked around until I felt something hard in the ashes. It turned out to be the blue bottle Amiel had given me, melted into a bent sapphire clump, the neck curved forward and open in a strange fish mouth of need.

Show me, I begged the bottle without speaking. I willed it to be a magic crystal ball that knew everything and fixed all.

"What's that?" my mother asked. She'd followed me into the grove, so I held out the bottle. Her hands were black and dry, like my mind.

"Just something I found," I said, and then, trying to restore my old talent for blurting out the truth, said, "He gave it to me once. Amiel."

The truth made it no easier for us to talk, and she looked like she would gladly have thrown the bottle into another fire.

While I was in the hospital, and then after I came home, newspaper stories kept giving us the numbers: 347,000 acres burned in San Diego County, 9,000 acres in Fallbrook and Rainbow, 21,000 avocado trees, winds in excess of eighty miles per hour, 1,700 homes, ten to fourteen lives, depending on whether the four bodies found in a migrant camp near Mexico were attributed to fire.

I heard tires moving slowly along the frontage road, and I silently begged the car not to contain my aunt and Robby. It was just another family of strangers out gawking at the damage, though. As the mother, the father, and two children watched us sift through bits of rubbish, I thought it was even worse than living in a house that was upside down, and I suddenly laughed out loud.

"What?" my mother asked.

"It's like we're hobos," I said. "Picking through the trash." I waved, and the passengers looked away.

I wanted, when I felt the ability to want anything besides

not having killed my uncle, to go to the river and look for Amiel.

"I want to go for a walk," I told my mother, holding the melted bottle in my dirty hand.

"No," my mother said.

"Don't you think we should go down where they found him and lay some flowers or something?" I'd thought about one of those crosses people put up at the sites of car accidents. But of course my mother knew that wasn't all.

"The cemetery is the place for that," she said.

"He's not *at* the cemetery." We still had the funeral ahead of us: tomorrow or the next day.

"When he is," she said.

"I have to go see if he's all right," I said, meaning Amiel this time.

"No, you don't," my mother said.

"I hate you," I said, shocking myself.

"Fine," my mother said.

We left holding a bowl, three forks, two spoons, the melted bottle, and the blobs of chrome.

Fifty-six

My mother didn't even listen to my arguments about why it would be better for me to stay home and get a GED than to go back to the high school when it opened.

"I can't face people," I said.

"If you can face me," she said, "you can face them."

I proposed moving out of town. "Like we could afford to move," she said.

So when school resumed after the evacuation, I resumed going there. Robby remained at the Gaudets' in Solana Beach while, as I heard from my mother, Agnès sought to enroll him at the Bishop's School, where he was soon thereafter accepted on scholarship.

"We're so sorry about your uncle," teachers and parents at school said to me if they addressed the subject at all, but mostly they didn't.

I knew they knew from a series of newspaper articles that Hoyt Wallace, age fifty-two, died trying to get out of the riverbed while he was looking for his niece, who was found in the company of a Hispanic male who fled. I assumed they also read the story in which a San Diego Gas and Electric employee said utility crews working to restore power to the Willow Glen area found evidence of human habitation and fire building in the preserve, which was highly illegal. These things they knew. They didn't know, and it didn't help anyone, that I walked around with the image of his burned body in front of my eye like those blobs that sometimes get stuck on the cornea or that I fervently prayed he died of smoke inhalation before he burned.

"So, Pearl?" various friends and not-friends asked. "Who were you with at the river?"

"I can't really talk," I said, whispering as though my own voice were too damaged to explain the many things that would, if told, exonerate me.

Greenie never asked about that or anything personal again, and though I saw her in the halls and at all the places you'd normally see someone who lived in your town, we either pretended not to notice one another or smiled fake smiles and waved as if we'd once shared nothing more than a few homeroom classes a long time ago when we were other people.

On the horrible sunny day of the funeral, my mother and I didn't sit by Robby or my aunt, who were naturally near the front. I continued to feign muteness, and my mother, though she knew better, didn't wise anybody up. She sat beside me at the back even though she was the barefoot girl in the biggest picture that was displayed at the front of the funeral chapel, the one photograph of Hoyt with my mother that hadn't burned, saved among various other family things by a cousin in Idaho. It showed a fifteen-year-old Hoyt and a five-year-old Sharon Wallace on Hoyt's first motorcycle. He's smiling and she's smiling, and they look like they're about to go off on a helmetless ride.

My father sent flowers, but he didn't come.

Robby played something by Mozart on the clarinet, and my aunt, who sat next to several unfamiliar French relatives, nodded when a slim bearded man said he was going to read a stanza from a poem by Agnès's favorite author, Victor Hugo.

"When the living leave us, moved, I gaze," he began, and though I kept my eyes focused on my fingers in my lap, I saw the mountain lion turn toward me in the smoke.

The breeze that takes you lifts me up alive,

And I'll follow those I loved.

The casket was closed. It lay huge and shiny on a bier at the front of the chapel. I watched for Mary Beth, who I thought would surely come to offer her respects to Robby if not to mourn, secretly, for Hoyt. I thought that Agnès was lucky in one thing: Hoyt hadn't left her for his lover as my father had left us. That was better, wasn't it? I knew what he'd done, and Robby knew, but Agnès didn't, and I added this to all the other qualities that made my uncle a good man.

Mitchell the marine was waiting respectfully outside for my mother. He was wearing camouflage, which he apologized for, and he'd come there on, of all things, a motorcycle. "So you're Pearl," he said, and I didn't hear any particular judgment in his voice, no more than I heard in other voices.

I could feel Robby and Agnès and the French contingent watching us and wondering about the soldier. I could do nothing but nod my frozen nod.

"Would you like me to go to the cemetery with you?" he asked my mother.

She was not only red-eyed and trembling but unable to speak. I think what she would really have liked was to ride on the back of his motorcycle to a place far away, as she had once done when she was five and Hoyt was fifteen, but she didn't do that. She led Mitchell to the Oyster car, and she handed him the keys, and understanding everything perfectly, he drove.

Fifty-seven

On Saturday, Mitchell came to the RV on his motorcycle. This time, he wasn't wearing his uniform. This time, my mother climbed on the back, locked her arms around his waist, and left me, against her better judgment, alone.

Thirty minutes and nine days after the fire started, I stood on the bank that once led to Amiel. It wasn't quiet. A cracking, pounding sound came from the grotto, and when I waded across, I found two men and a woman whacking the shell of Amiel's hut with sledgehammers.

They stopped and stared suspiciously at me.

"What are you doing?" I asked. I surprised even myself with my loud, undamaged voice.

"Removing a fire hazard," they said.

I didn't go past them to the roofless homesteader's house for fear I'd lead them to something they hadn't yet discovered.

I'd have to find another way. I walked downstream, then worked my way around, got lost, and finally recognized the sycamore that led to the front door. I climbed up and stood under trees dry and rattly in the blue air, terrified that once I entered the house, what I'd find would be a corpse like my uncle's.

You knew who, the doves in the trees chided. *You knew who knew.*

I stepped in. The foundation was clean, just as we'd left it, except for ash. Ash lay over everything. I walked all over the foundation raising little puffs of it with my shoes, looking for a trail that would show me where he'd gone. In one corner, I startled a lizard with a missing tail. A phoebe sat on a stump outside the doorway, waiting for something in her black coat. Nothing in the house seemed left there for me, but I kept walking over the floor and listening to the sledgehammers.

"Ready for lunch?" I heard one of the men say.

"After I get this sucker out," the other called.

Then I saw it. Amiel's writing stick, the one he'd balanced upright in his palm, lay against the wall in some leaves, and when I pulled it out, a piece of paper that had been coiled around the tip loosened and dropped. Unfurled, it said *BLACK OAK.*

"Where did that girl go?" the woman asked the men who were smashing things.

"I don't know."

"Do you think she's the one?"

I ducked down and crept along the far edge of the willows

until I reached a point where I could wade across the shallow river. I saw the woman's red bandanna as she dipped down to wet her hands, and I saw her regard me dubiously, but I kept going as if I didn't care.

There, in the hollow of the burned oak, sat the pale green and black tin. There were the lords and ladies, the filigree, the lute. With shaking, smudgy fingers, I picked off the lid. Under a drawing of an oyster shell and a pearl, Amiel had written:

Vuelvo a México. Recuérdeme.

Simple enough for even me: *I'm going back to Mexico. Remember me.*

I had another stop to make, and I took the tin and Amiel's stick with me.

Recuérdeme. The four syllables formed a rhythm in my sick heart. I had to go past the sledgehammer crew again, past the green canopy into the burn zone. Under my feet the hard dirt became thick, powdery ash. *Recuérdeme.* Black manzanita twisted out of the slopes beneath black oak. Black oak lay down against black sycamore. The plants the boy called hobo pineapples poked fresh and green out of the black earth. I was getting closer now to Willow Glen, closer to the spot where my uncle, according to the description in the paper, had decided to go uphill to get away from the fire. I was wondering how I would know I was there when I saw the roses.

It wasn't that far from where we'd eaten the loquats. The trees, though burned, still arched above me. Black and white and gray, like snowy woods in winter. And there on the northern slope I saw pile after pile of roses, each bouquet successively older and drier, so that the fresh bunch was still bright red, the one just beneath it dried red and wrinkly, others yellow, some pink, all of them long-stemmed and wrapped with a ribbon like florists use. Among the roses were other things that people had left. One card was signed by the Fallbrook fire department. Another said, *A hiker who wishes you well.*

Just above the flowers was a wooden cross that had a set of GPS numbers written on it in white ink. Someone—Agnès, I supposed—had tacked a photograph of Hoyt to the cross, and I saw that it was a picture of Hoyt and Robby at Robby's seventeenth birthday party. My uncle glowed in the twilight like the peaceful ghost I wanted him to be as I knelt down in the ash by the flowers and covered my blue eye instead of the brown one.

"I can't really see you, Hoyt," I said, crying as I couldn't cry at the funeral. "I can't."

Still kneeling in the ashes, I took Amiel's stick and started to write in the dust that was so fine I could feel it rising up to smother me, *I'm sorry Robby I'm sorry Agnès I'm sorry Hoyt I'm sorry Mom,* but they were not the right words to make the invisible appear, and after a while I had no choice but to walk out.

Fifty-eight

A whole year passed before Mary Beth Fowler came up to me at a Fallbrook High football game and said, "Hi, Pearl."

I stared at her for a second, stunned, and then at the backs of the girls sitting in front of us. I no longer had any claim to muteness, so I said, "Hi."

"I'm sorry about your uncle," she said.

This I never answer anymore.

"You know that Robby told me not to come to the funeral, right?" she said, her hair cut short and brushing against her turtleneck but her face still innocently, childishly pretty.

"No. I didn't. I looked for you, actually."

"He acted like it would be really offensive for me to be there, which I didn't get."

I hoped that something would interrupt us, such as the

cheerleaders asking our section to do the wave. "I guess he just thought it would be weird for you to be there," I said.

"Why would it be weird?"

"Because of your relationship with his dad."

Mary Beth stared at me. She didn't look embarrassed or guilty, just confused. "What are you talking about?" she asked.

"You and my uncle—the affair. Robby knew." On the field, among the bright red and blue shirts, play resumed.

Mary Beth turned a sort of plum color. "There wasn't an *affair*."

"But he saw you. At the house. Kissing his dad. I guess he was hiding in the bushes trying to figure out why his dad was acting so odd."

She tugged at her sleeves as everyone around us jumped up and screamed about a play that we weren't watching.

When they were quiet enough for her to continue, she told me she knew what day I was talking about, but he had it all wrong. She said she came out to the house to drop off a tennis racket she'd gotten re-strung for Mrs. Wallace. Nobody was home but Hoyt, and he offered her a Coke. They started talking in the kitchen about Paris because Mary Beth was saving up to go there, and he wanted to recommend an apartment his wife's cousin rented out near the Eiffel Tower.

"He thought he had the address and stuff in his room, in a box, and he told me to come on upstairs, and I remember thinking I shouldn't go into his room, but if I acted like it was a big deal, then it would *be* a big deal. So I acted like it was nothing, and while he's going through the box, showing me stuff, I hear the front door open and shut, and I'm thinking, 'Oh my God! Agnès is home! What's she going to think?' Mr. Wallace thought the same thing, so we're like in some sort of play with all these doors opening and shutting. It was kind of funny, but it was incredibly stressful, too, especially when Robby came to the door.

"Anyway, Robby left, or I thought he left, and Mr. Wallace walked me to my car. When we get there, he goes, 'Well, *that* was a lot of trouble to prevent the appearance of something that couldn't possibly happen.' "

Mary Beth paused for an unnaturally long time, and she looked into the distance where the other team sat and pressed her thumbnail against her lip.

"This is really hard to explain," she said at last. "I don't know if I should even try."

I didn't want to hear anything bad about my uncle, and that's how the story was starting to sound. I just waited.

"Okay," Mary Beth said. "You're probably not going to believe me, but this really is the truth. I said to Mr. Wallace, '*What* couldn't possibly happen?' and he said, 'Who would believe that a beautiful girl like you would be running around with an old muttonchop like me?' He looked kind of sad, you know, and I said, 'It's not *that* impossible,' and I went to hug him, which I guess was the wrong move. He thought I was going to kiss him, so our lips met, but it was not a passionate kiss at all, more like one of those greetings or farewells where you're just planning to shake hands or hug but the other person is doing some French thing, first one cheek and then the other."

I listened to all this while players were smacking and darting across the football field and the cheerleaders were shouting, "Let's go, Warriors, let's go!" Mary Beth watched the football players for a second after she finished the story.

"Do you believe me?" she asked.

"Yeah," I said, relieved that what she'd brought to me was a better version of my uncle, the one he'd always seemed to be. "I do."

"Thanks," she said.

"You should tell Robby," I said.

"Yeah," she said, staring at the field for a while. Then she shook her head. "I don't think I could after all that's happened. After the funeral, which like I said, he told me not to attend, I just decided Rob was a psycho, that he was one of those weird people who want something until they've got it, and then they don't want it anymore. He really, really hurt me."

I just sat there.

"Maybe *you* could tell him," she said. "He'd believe you."

"Me? He doesn't talk to me anymore. I'm the last person he would believe."

She gave me a look of genuine surprise. "Why not?"

"Don't you know?" I said. "Because it was my fault that Hoyt was—that he died."

Except for the therapist my mother made me see, no one ever knows what to say to this, and Mary Beth didn't, either. Dr. Daggett says I went down into the burning riverbed to get my father's attention. Therefore, according to Dr. Daggett's line of reasoning, it was my father's fault that my uncle died. I never believe this.

Mary Beth watched the final play of the game in the unseeing way that I observed all sports—and most other things—and then the game was over and we lost. She touched my hand, putting pressure on it in a way that let me know she was trying to say she was sorry but couldn't think how. "Take care," she said, and walked down the bleachers to the friendly-looking guy who was waving to her from the sidelines, and I never saw her again.

A month or so later, I wrote two letters—the real thing, handwritten, pen and paper. The first was to Robby and repeated Mary Beth's story. The second was to my aunt Agnès and said that I knew she could never forgive me, that I didn't forgive myself, but I wanted to tell her that I knew it was my fault that my uncle died in the fire.

Six weeks or so went by and we received a postcard with a picture of the Tuileries on the front. The postcard was addressed to my mother, not me, and it said, *Dear Aunt Sharon, Please thank your daughter for the informative letter. R.*

I looked at the postcard several times before it occurred to me that in addition to pretending I didn't exist, he must have decided never to say or write my name.

A little while after that, one of my aunt Agnès's monogrammed envelopes, cream-colored and heavy and smooth, appeared in the mailbox. When I opened it, her perfume wafted out like a ghost.

Dear Pearl, it said. *Faute avouée est à moitié pardonnée.*

She didn't translate, but I managed to look it up and be comforted a little by her belief that a fault acknowledged is halfway forgiven. I might write to her sometime and tell her that I've pinned lines from the Victor Hugo poem above my desk and that they have helped me plan the future:

> *The breeze that takes you lifts me up alive,*
> *And I'll follow those I loved, I the exile.*

Fifty-nine

It's spring again, two months from graduation. I take night classes in botany and Spanish and work for an hourly wage that goes directly to the bank. By September, it will be enough for a Spanish immersion program at an institute two hours from a town that has a bus to San Ygnacio, Guanajuato. I'll go from San Miguel to Silao and from there to the dirt road a former employee of my uncle's has described to me as *muy, muy larga* and lined on one side with *guayaba* trees. When I see the church of San Ygnacio, I'll get out and begin to ask, "Do you know Amiel de la Cruz Guerrero?" If the men and women shake their heads, I'll find a tree with wide branches and take my place in the shade until the children creep forward. Then I'll point to my eyes and say that I see into this world and the next, and I'm looking for one who has passed over *la frontera* and returned home. He speaks little and works in the fields. He lives in a house on the hill. Sometimes at night you will see him on his porch painted turquoise, looking out, sitting alone with two empty chairs. Do you know him?

ACKNOWLEDGMENTS

With particular thanks to John Hayek, Todd and Bia Jackson, Josh Krimston, Kathy Lambert, Jeff Lucia, Candido Rocha, and Diane and Bailey Wilson. What you knew, you shared with me. I am also indebted to Joan Slattery, Allison Wortche, George Nicholson, and, from beginning to end, to Tom.

ABOUT THE AUTHOR

Laura Rhoton McNeal holds a master's degree in fiction writing from Syracuse University. She taught middle school and high school English before becoming a novelist and journalist.

Together, Laura and her husband, Tom McNeal, are the authors of *Crooked*, winner of the California Book Award for Juvenile Literature and an ALA Top Ten Best Book for Young Adults; *Zipped*, winner of the PEN Center USA Literary Award for Children's Literature; *Crushed* (called "compelling" by *Publishers Weekly*); and *The Decoding of Lana Morris*, a *Kirkus Reviews* Best Young Adult Book of the Year.

The McNeals live in Southern California with their two sons, Sam and Hank. To learn more, please visit the authors' Web site at www.mcnealbooks.com.